KARMA
AND
EVE

Karma and Eve Book 1
© 2024 by D McLoughlin
Illustrations © 2024 by AC Cable

Crimson Pine Publishing crimsonpinepublishing.com

ISBN: 978-1-0690524-0-7

Library of Congress Cataloging-in-Publication Data *Karma and Eve Book 1* / D McLoughlin; illustrated by AC Cable. p. cm.
Includes bibliographical references and index.
ISBN 978-1-0690524-0-7

1. American coming of age—Fiction. 2. Mental health—Fiction. 3. Crime—Fiction. I. Karma and Eve.

Printed in Baltimore, Maryland
United States of America

First Edition: 2024

Cover design by AC Cable Illustrations by AC Cable
This is a work of fiction. Names, characters, places, and incidents are either the product of the author's imagination or used fictitiously. Any resemblance to actual persons, living or dead, events, or locales is entirely coincidental.

D McLOUGHLIN

Writer

AC CABLE

Illustrator

KARMA AND EVE

Preface

This story follows Karma and Eve, two young women bound by scars both visible and hidden. They meet within the walls of Helmbrook, a mental institution, and form a connection that defies the rules and expectations society has set for them. Together, they break free, launching into a world that both terrifies and excites them, fueled by drugs and their drive to find meaning, revenge, and maybe even redemption.

Karma and Eve is not a tale of heroes. It's a story about survival, about holding on when everything else fades, and about two souls fighting against a world that labels them as dangerous and unworthy.

This book was born from a desire to tell the kind of story that doesn't flinch at darkness but dares to explore the broken and the defiant, side by side.

KARMA AND EVE

KARMA AND EVE

KARMA AND EVE

BOOK 1

Written by
D McLOUGLIN

Art by
AC CABLE

10 9 8 7 6
1 2 3 4 5
FORGET

CHAPTER 1

OUT OF DARKNESS

Karma lay submerged in the warm, murky bathwater, her dyed black hair fanning like dark tendrils around her neck. Streaks of smeared eye makeup trailed down her cheeks like ink bleeding from a broken pen and mingled with the tears that had left her eyes raw and swollen from hours of crying. Her breath was ragged and uneven. She drew in a slow inhale, holding it as she sank beneath the surface.

A single bubble escaped from her nostril, twisting its way upward through the fragile and fleeting water before breaking at the surface.

An unshaded bulb dangled from the ceiling, its weak glow casting a long shadow across the cramped room, resembling a dark, skeletal finger. With its chipped white enamel, the clawfoot tub revealed the cast iron beneath and dominated the center of the room. Karma's pale skin was almost translucent against the dirty water, enveloping her as a cocoon, muffling the sounds of the world outside. Bubbles clung to her like shimmering jewels, reflecting the dim light. Her heartbeat pounded in her ears, a stark reminder that she was still painfully alive.

Lost in dark thoughts, she began to count silently, a ritual she had previously used to ground herself. "One, two, three..."

She burst to the surface with a gasp, water sloshing around her, but she could not catch her breath as the cold air hit her face.

A sharp cough wracked her body, forcing her to gulp for air.

Karma's hands shuttered as she frantically clawed at the rim of the tub, her fingers digging into the porcelain, nails scraping against the slick surface, desperate to find some grip. She rested for a moment, gathering herself. Her breathing was shallow and ragged as she clung to the tub's edge, her knuckles white against the porcelain.

Karma leaned over, her hand reaching down, causing water to spill from the tub. Tiny puddles formed along the grout lines of the cracked octagonal tiles, the black-and-white checkerboard pattern stretching across the worn floor.

Her fingers brushed against a folded straight blade she'd swiped from her father's bathroom hours earlier. She picked it up, its cold weight unsettling in her palm, then leaned back into the tub. Her pale fingers trembled as she unfolded the blade, the soft click of the metal hinge echoing in the stillness.

Her silhouette glided above the porcelain bottom, pubic hair floating around her crotch like seaweed peering out of the ocean. Her breasts swayed gently, nipples firm, reaching toward the faint moonlight filtering through the tiny skylight, casting an incredible, silvery sheen across her skin. Out of the corner of her eye, she spotted a giant spider creeping along the bathroom wall. Each leg extended with a calculated, graceful precision. The spider's dark, bulbous body glistened faintly; its many eyes reflected the light with an eerie shimmer. She watched intently, her stoned eyes tracking its every step, entranced by the creature's slow, steady crawl. Shifting her toe, she lifted her foot from the water. She twisted the faucet knob, sending a fresh stream into the nearly overflowing tub. The razor's handle was tightly clenched in her right hand, and she pressed the cool, sharp edge with steady force against her wrist. Her body tensed as she hesitated, flickering with uncertainty before she flinched, exhaled, and allowed her muscles to relax.

In one swift, fluid motion, the blade cut through her skin, and a thin trickle of blood quickly bloomed into a deep, steady flow. A sudden, unexpected wave of arousal coursed through her body, merging with the warm calm that washed over her. Karma stared, transfixed, as the blood swirled into the water, turning it a grimy reddish-brown. The sight held her in its grasp, both soothing and strangely hypnotic, like a dark ribbon unraveling in the depths.

As she watched, her eyelids grew heavy, and the pull of sleep became irresistible as her body began to succumb to the shock of losing all that blood. Her eyes slowly drifted shut, sinking into the quiet darkness with the same slow, winding grace as though she were being gently pulled under.

Meanwhile, downstairs.

The ground floor smelled rich and earthy, and the air was filled with Mediterranean scents that enveloped the old, gothic brownstone, swirling around the ornate wooden banisters and intricate colonial moldings.

Vic Papadakis sat at the head of the long wooden dinner table, surrounded by the sounds of family chatter and the rich aroma of roasted lamb. He reached for the rustic jug of wine, pouring the deep red liquid into his stemmed glass with a slow, practiced motion. Lifting his glass to his mouth, Vic nodded toward Uncle Theo, whose fingers plucked effortlessly over the bouzouki strings, filling the room with music. He sipped the wine, then grinned as he raised his glass in a toast. The flickering candlelight danced in the ruby liquid, which clinked softly amidst the warm, lively atmosphere.

"To our health and the love of family!" he said in Greek.

"Στην υγειά μας και στην αγάπη της οικογένειας!"

Theo lifted his glass, raising it toward Vic, then polished off his drink before returning to his bouzouki.

"Play that one again, Theo!" Vic called out, his voice slightly slurred. "It always reminds me of Greece."

"In every breath of love, in the land of Greece, the stars shine, pure light, and melt hearts. In the sea and the sky, I find your glance, with the wave I sing, I love you forever. At every step in life, my Greece and you."

Eight-year-old Antoinette knelt beside Vic, her dark, curly hair cascading over her shoulders. The soft light bathed her olive-toned skin in warmth, and her large, expressive eyes sparkled with quiet, innocent joy. She entertained herself by threading her tiny fingers through Uncle Theo's shoelaces, smiling and singing along under her breath.

Theo's fingers danced over the strings, drawing out a melody. After a moment, he paused, reached for the jug of homemade wine, and filled his glass. He lifted it, swirling the wine before taking a slow sip. With a quiet nod, he set the glass back on the corner of the table and resumed playing the song. *"In the language of love,"* Theo sang, his voice warm like the sun dipping below the horizon, soft and golden. His fingers moved across the strings, playing a melody that seemed to rise from the depths of his soul.

"Love, love, sweet love," he continued to sing.

Ophelia, Vic's wife and devoted mother of Karma and Antoinette, wore a warm, radiant smile as she moved through the room with quiet grace. Her presence was both confident and gentle. The contours of her face, a perfect blend of sharp angles and soft curves, reflected her distinctive mix of Greek and American heritage. The air seemed to settle when she was near, putting those around her at ease. It wasn't just her kindness that drew people in—it was how she lived her life, rooted in family, loyalty, and love.

But beneath that calm, another story was whispered behind closed doors. How could a woman so full of light be bound to someone like Vic? His charm concealed something darker, something lurking just beneath the surface. Vic wasn't a kingpin; he didn't control the entire underworld but led a small, tight-knit group known as "The Greeks." They made their money in shady ways—more minor crimes that kept them under the radar yet still connected to more prominent, dangerous players. They were organized, mob-adjacent, operating in the shadows of the city. And yet, she lived with that darkness, married to a man whose world thrived on secrets and quiet corruption.

With careful hands, she placed the tray on the cluttered table. Vic's mother, Sofia, a petite Greek immigrant, followed closely behind. Despite her age, she moved quickly, carrying a large tray of side dishes that accompanied the enormous piece of lamb the local butcher had delivered earlier that afternoon. The air was filled with an irresistible aroma—salad tossed with feta, soutzoukakia, fragrant herbs, moussaka, and golden-brown pita bread, still warm and impossibly tempting.

Sophia leaned toward Uncle Theo, her voice soft but steady. "Your music brings life to this table," she said in her thick Greek accent. "It fills our hearts with joy and connects us to our roots."

"My pleasure, Aunt Sophia," Theo replied, grinning, his wine-stained teeth showing.

"Where's Karma?" Vic asked, his eyes scanning the room with a sharp edge.

"She's in the bath," Antoinette replied from Uncle Theo's feet, not bothering to look up.

Vic's voice hardened. "No." He swilled back the rest of his wine.

"Get her down here now; dinner's ready."

Ding-dong.

Before anyone could move, the doorbell chimed, cutting through the room and diffusing the tension about to ignite as the conversation went cold.

"Antoinette jumped to her feet, eager to escape the sudden shift. 'I'll get it!' she called halfway to the door. Vic's hand came down firmly on the table, his voice leaving no room for debate.

"No, you go get your sister."

Antoinette stopped, looking back at him, knowing better than to argue.

"I'll handle the door," Ophelia said, her voice gentle yet commanding as she patted Antoinette's head.

"Come on now, let's move," she added with a light smile, clapping her hands and gently nudging Antoinette toward the stairs.

Ophelia walked to the door, untying her apron and folding it neatly into a tight ball. She paused momentarily, her gaze catching the mirror by the entrance. She studied her reflection, adjusting her hair and smoothing her blouse with a quick, practiced touch before turning to answer the door. Antoinette dashed to the stairs, her footsteps tapping on the hardwood floors. The click of her black pleather shoes created a rhythmic beat as she hurried up the staircase.

"Karmela?" she called out, her voice carrying through the house. Reaching the top of the stairs, she let go of the rickety wooden handrail and stepped onto the worn runner carpet. Her footsteps softened against the faded fabric as she moved cautiously down the dimly lit corridor.

"Karmela!" she called again, her small shadow stretching long across the wall as she approached the door. She paused, noticing the soft light spilling from the crack beneath the bathroom door frame.

With a gentle knock, her knuckles made a quiet tap against the wood—tap, tap, tap.

"It's dinner time. We're waiting for you!" Antoinette yelled.

She could faintly hear the sound of the tub filling on the other side. She knocked again, her knuckles tapping harder against the door. Rap-rap-rap.

Her anxiety grew with each passing second. Glancing down, she noticed water slowly creeping from under the door.

"Karma!" Antoinette yelled, louder now, her voice

strained, fear tightening around each word. Shifting uneasily, she lifted her feet to avoid the water creeping toward her, the puddle growing beneath the door and under her feet.

At first, her hand fumbled with the doorknob, shaking it as she tried to get a grip. Finally, she twisted it open, and the door swung wide, sending a thin, layered rush of water spilling across the floor. Hot, steamy air slammed into her face, thick with the sharp, metallic scent of iron. It clung to her skin, and instantly, she knew something was wrong.

Antoinette's heart pounded against her chest.

"AAAAAAAAAHHHHHHHH!" The scream tore from her throat, raw and primal, her face twisted in horror as her eyes locked onto the figure slumped in the tub. Her breath quickened, each gasp more frantic than the last, her chest heaving as panic clawed its way in.

Karma's lifeless body lay half-submerged, eyes closed as if in a restless sleep, with one arm hanging limply over the edge. Crimson ribbons of blood trickled from her wrist, bleeding into the water, swirling and spreading in delicate patterns. Antoinette stood frozen, her feet rooted to the spot. Her mind screamed at her to move, but her body refused to obey.

"AAAAAAAAAAAAAAAHHHHHHHHHH!"

Her scream reverberated through the house, filling every corner with raw terror. Footsteps pounded up the stairs behind her, crashing against the hardwood with increasing speed and urgency, each step louder, faster, more frantic, as if the whole house trembled under the weight of panic.

"Antoinette!" Ophelia's voice shrieked from below. "Are you okay?! What happened?!"

Vic's booming voice followed, "What the hell is going on up there?"

Antoinette stood frozen in the doorway, tears streaming down her face, her body trembling as panic overwhelmed her mind. The hallway shook as they raced toward her, footsteps pounding like thunder echoing through the hall.

They reached the bathroom, and Ophelia's scream tore through the air at the horrifying sight. Instinctively, she pulled Antoinette close, shielding her eyes from the scene unfolding before them.

Vic's face went pale as he pushed them behind him, his voice rough and filled with panic. "Get her out of here! Take Antoinette away—now!" he barked, his words urgent, almost shaking with fear.

CHAPTER 2

HELLBROOK

One Month Later

Ophelia, Vic, Antoinette, and Karma moved through the crowded halls of Bayview Medical Center, their steps awkward and out of sync. Karma had been locked away in a sterile room, under constant watch, ever since the suicide attempt. Now, she was finally getting out, a wave of relief washing over her—but it was tainted by the fact that she had to leave with her family. Suspicion gnawed at her, though. Even though they were heading toward the exit, she couldn't shake the uneasy feeling that they might not be going home after all.

The sliding glass doors whooshed open, releasing them into late afternoon's thick, stifling heat. The change was abrupt—cool; air-conditioned air gave way to heavy humidity that clung to their skin. The heat pressed down on them like a suffocating blanket as they trudged across the crowded parking lot, the sun's harsh glare bouncing off the asphalt, leading them toward the familiar sight of the family Oldsmobile.

They reached the car, and with a sharp, mechanical click, Vic unlocked the doors. Antoinette slid into the backseat next to Karma, her gaze flickering nervously between her sister and their parents.

Ophelia pulled the door shut with a soft thud and settled into the passenger seat, her fingers tightly gripping her purse strap.

Chug-chug... vroom, the engine came to life, sputtering and groaning with age as it coughed up thick clouds of exhaust and sat idling for a moment. He took a sharp breath, exhaling slowly before shifting into reverse and carefully guiding the Oldsmobile out of the tight parking spot.

His eyes darted between the rearview and side mirrors, navigating the cramped space. The car crept backward, inching along slowly, until he had enough room to straighten the wheel.

"Diáole aftó eínai ntropiastikó," Vic muttered under his breath.

Ophelia tapped him with the back of her hand for swearing in Greek, but he ignored her, his eyes locked on the road. Vic shifted into drive, rolling forward slowly as he eased on the gas. Just as the car began to pick up speed, a pedestrian stepped off the curb, appearing out of nowhere and walking directly into his path.

Vic slammed on the brakes.

The tires shrieked against the asphalt, their piercing screech slicing through the air as the car jolted to a violent stop. Karma's face went pale, her muscles tensing as she braced for impact. The sudden force yanked everyone back into their seats, seat belts digging into their chests, leaving them breathless, shaken, and hearts pounding in the abrupt stillness. Vic's gaze locked onto the pedestrian—an older woman who had stumbled back onto the sidewalk, her expression a mix of shock and confusion. "Watch where you're going, jerk!" she shouted, her voice brimming with outrage.

"Γάμησε τη μάνα σου!" Vic barked back at her, leaning out the open window, eyes fixed on her.

"Vic!" Ophelia hissed, swatting his shoulder. "The girls! I've already told you."

"They don't understand Greek," he muttered, glaring at the old woman.

"They have eyes," Ophelia said and shot him a sharp look, then glanced pointedly at Antoinette, who was watching the exchange.

"Jesus, Dad!" Karma snapped from the backseat.

"You say I'm the reckless one—look at you, you almost killed that old lady!"

"Quiet, Karmela," Ophelia warned, turning in her seat to glare at her.

"Don't start."

Karma rolled her eyes, slumping back in her seat as she twisted the bandages on her wrists. She stared out the window, her voice low and layered in defiance.

"Yeah, whatever."

Vic's hands tightened on the wheel, his jaw clenched.

"Just shut up, Karma," he muttered, his voice barely audible over the engine's rumble.

He yanked the car out of the lot and merged aggressively into the stream of traffic. Ophelia sat stiffly beside him, her gaze fixed on the horizon as the city blurred into the distance. Antoinette's face was bathed in cool daylight in the backseat, her nose buried in a worn copy of a teen-pop magazine. Beside her, Karma stared out the window, her thoughts drifting as far as the rolling landscape.

Time passed slowly as the Oldsmobile rumbled along the highway, its V8 engine humming with a steady, familiar rhythm. Outside the windows, the world seemed to drift by in slow, languid waves. Rolling meadows stretched into the distance, dotted with patches of wildflowers, their bright colors muted by the lengthening shadows of early evening. The silence inside the car felt heavy, and then Karma finally spoke.

"Where are we going? Why aren't we heading home?" she asked, her voice cutting through the stillness, suspicion creeping into her tone.

Everyone stayed low, their eyes avoiding one another. The Oldsmobile continued down the highway, the landscape rolling endlessly by.

The road twisted ahead as they pulled off exit US-113. The Oldsmobile dipped and swayed with each bend, trees along the roadside thickening, their shadows stretching across the asphalt. The drive carried them deeper into Selbyville, Delaware—a small town surrounded by groves and farmlands. The air felt heavier here, and the silence inside the car grew even more suffocating as they moved further into the countryside. Tall oaks and maples lined the road, their leaves swaying gently in the summer breeze. The Baltimore skyline had long faded from view, replaced by the quiet expanse of rolling meadows and fields.

Every bump in the road seemed to intensify the tension, making the silence in the car feel even heavier. Vic stayed quiet, puffing on a cigarette, the smoke curling toward the partially open window before being pulled into the humid air. His frustration simmered just beneath the surface, barely contained. He glanced at the rearview mirror, briefly examining Karma's expressionless face. A hint of worry crossed his eyes, but the tension quickly swallowed it up. He turned his attention back to the road, exhaling another plume of smoke.

"Do you have any idea how embarrassing this is?" Vic's voice was sharp, cutting through the silence. "How bad this makes our family look?" he snapped, his words tight with anger, each one like a blade.

"She knows, she knows," Ophelia interjected quickly,

trying to defuse the tension. "Stop it, Vic."

Karma pressed her face against the cool glass of the backseat window, tuning out the argument. Antoinette reached over, her hand brushing against Karma's in a gesture of concern. But Karma pulled away, her expression hardening.

"Now's not the time for this," Ophelia said, glancing at Karma before forcing a smile for Antoinette's sake.

"It is the time!" Vic's frustration boiled over as he turned slightly in his seat, locked eyes with Ophelia and raised his voice.

"Just stop, Vic," she said, her voice strained, trying to calm the tension before it worsened.

"She's a drug addict!" His hand slammed against the steering wheel, the thud echoing through the car, making everyone flinch. "They were my pills," Ophelia shot back. "I shouldn't have given them to her for her cramps."

"And now she's a thief, too?" His voice escalated, anger bubbling closer to the surface.

"All kids do things like this." She reiterated. Vic's face reddened with rage, and his voice cracked as he shouted, "Karmela tried to kill herself! Do you not get that?

She's sick in the head!"

"It was an accident, Vic."

"Enough!" he barked, cutting her off. "I don't want to hear this crap anymore."

"This is our daughter, Victor!" she yelled, her voice

breaking. Vic drew in a ragged breath, his chest heaving as he fought to steady himself. Karma curled into the corner of her seat, her hoodie pulled low like a shield. She stared blankly out the window, her body tense and withdrawn, wishing she could disappear— just anywhere but here, anywhere but near Vic. Ophelia reached out, her hand resting gently on Karma's arm, rubbing her fingers softly against her daughter's skin to offer comfort. But Karma barely acknowledged her, throwing her mother a sideways glance before pulling away.

The car jolted over a speed bump, sending them all lurching forward like rag dolls, but they kept moving without slowing down. As they scrambled to steady themselves, Karma's voice cut through the air, dripping with sarcasm.

"Great driving, Vic."

He ignored her jab and accelerated down the facility's narrow road.

"You have everything, Karma," Vic muttered, his voice quieter now but filled with resentment. "I don't understand why you do these things."

The car sped past a weathered, rusted sign, its once-bright letters now dulled by years of neglect:

Helmbrook Psychiatric Center

Restoring Minds, Renewing Lives

Since 1952

The facility loomed ahead—a cluster of whitewashed buildings stark against the overgrown, dull landscape. The structures stood cold and institutional, their walls weathered by time and streaked with grime from years of neglect. Barred windows dotted dark and imposing exteriors, casting sharp lines across the ground below. The buildings jutted into the horizon, their rigid lines and unforgiving angles giving off the appearance of a prison.

Around the facility, the grounds were equally bleak. A greenish-brown field stretched endlessly, dotted with patches of dried grass and stubborn weeds clawing at the earth. Towering oaks stood scattered across the property, their gnarled branches twisting toward the sky, casting long, eerie shadows over the cracked, uneven pavement. A chain-link fence bordered the property, topped with coils of rusted barbed wire, further emphasizing the sense of confinement. As the Oldsmobile came to a stop in front of one of the buildings.

An older man, a middle-aged woman, and two burly men in matching off-white scrubs stood waiting by the worn concrete steps leading up to a set of double doors. The men shifted on the cracked surface. One tapped his foot against the chipped edge, and the other leaned on the metal rail. The woman tightened her grip on a clipboard, her eyes flicking between the group and the doors.

"Alright, these are them." The woman said to the others. Antoinette peered out the back window, her big brown eyes locking onto the strangers who stood on the steps a few feet away, their expressions unreadable.

Vic opened the door and stepped out, followed by Ophelia, who helped Antoinette out of the back seat. Karma stayed slumped in her corner, hoodie pulled low, her eyes sharp but unfocused. She could feel it—something was coming, something she wouldn't like. Her insides tightened, coiling like a spring, readying to explode.

Dr. Conner, a middle-aged woman with a calm and reassuring demeanor, greeted them with a warm smile. She extended her hand toward Vic.

"Welcome to Helmbrook. I'm Dr. Conner."

Vic forced a polite smile.

"Hello, Dr. Conner. I'm Vic," he said, "This is my wife, Ophelia, our youngest, Antoinette... and Karma… in the car." Ophelia turned to Karma, her voice gentle yet persistent, attempting to calm the brewing storm.

"You can't stay in the car, Karma. Let's go."

Karma stirred slightly but remained planted, not even glancing their way.

"Out of the car!" Vic snapped, clapping his hands sharply.

"Come on, come on, no more bullshit!" he said and turned to Dr. Conner, "Excuse me."

"No," Karma barked, her voice icy and defiant. She sat rigid, arms crossed, shaking her head, eyes fixed on the dashboard, avoiding all of them.

Dr. Conner stepped forward cautiously, her tone gentle

and measured. "Hello, Karma. I'm Dr. Conner. I'd love for you to come in and chat with me."

Karma's eyes rolled. "Who the hell are you, bitch?" She said to her.

Dr. Conner didn't flinch, her expression steady and unreadable. She glanced at the two burly men beside her and quickly nodded. They moved in, pulling the back door open. The second they laid hands on Karma, she snapped. "What the hell, man!" Karma shouted, her body tightening, going rigid as a raw cry tore from her throat. She kicked, thrashed, and was wild, and the fury raged within her.

"Get off me, you fucks, I'm not going with you!"

"Please, Karma," Dr. Conner said, her tone steady but firm. "We're here to help."

Karma's voice echoed across the parking lot, sharp and desperate.

"No! I don't want this! You can't make me!"

Vic, Ophelia, and Antoinette stood frozen, helpless. Vic's jaw tightened, his teeth grinding together. Ophelia's eyes filled, her heart breaking as she watched her daughter being dragged from the car, helpless to intervene.

Suddenly, Antoinette burst into tears, her voice trembling as she cried out,

"No! Stop! You can't take her! She's my sister!"

Ophelia wrapped her arms around Antoinette, pulling her close. "It's okay, sweetheart," she whispered, though her voice shook, betraying her broken heart.

Karma's voice wavered with fear now, her wild eyes darting from face to face.

"What's happening? What are you doing? Let me go!" Her screams echoed through the air, her body thrashing in raw panic. The family stood frozen, helpless, their faces torn between heartbreak and the crushing weight of their powerlessness.

Suddenly, Antoinette broke down, her weak voice shaking.

"No! Stop! You can't take her! She's my sister!"

Ophelia pulled her close, whispering, "It's okay, sweetheart," though her heart broke.

Karma's voice cracked, her wild eyes darting in every direction.

"What's happening? What are you doing? Let me go!"

No one could stop it. Karma's family watched as the men dragged her away, their grips firm around Karma. Dr. Conner stepped forward; her voice was soft yet commanding.

"Karma, this is for your own good. We're trying to help you." Her panic escalated, her voice a desperate scream.

"I don't need your help!" Her body jerked harder. Tears poured down her face as she lashed out.

"Argh!"

Antoinette's tear-filled voice cut through the chaos. She grabbed Karma's arm, refusing to let go.

"Please, don't leave her here! Don't make her stay!"

Karma's voice turned into a raw plea, her desperation palpable. "Mom, Dad, please! I don't belong here. I can't stay… It's not fair! I need to go home!"

Dr. Conner raised her hand, motioning for the orderlies to ease up.

"Karma, it's alright," she said gently. "Please, calm down. We're here to help you."

Karma's wide, terrified eyes locked onto Dr. Conner's. The doctor's calmness pierced through the storm of her panic. Slowly, her struggles weakened, her breath became steady, and the fight left her body as she accepted the stillness.

"It's okay. You can let go now," Dr. Conner said softly.

She gestured for the orderlies to step back. "We're going to take this one step at a time. It's about trust, Karma."

The orderlies released her but stayed nearby, their faces stoic. Karma stood frozen, her chest rising and falling with each shaky breath. She glanced around the unfamiliar surroundings, her anger slowly reaching exhaustion.

Dr. Conner took a step closer. "Let's get you inside, Karma," she said gently. "It'll be okay. We'll just sit and talk." Karma hesitated, then nodded slightly. She wiped the tears from her face with the back of her hand, still trembling but no longer resisting. She took a tentative step forward, casting one last glance at her family before following Dr. Conner inside. Ophelia watched her daughter disappear through the doors, her heart heavy with what they had just done.

"Breathe, Karma. We're going to take this one step at a time."

The doctor reiterated.

As they walked down the hall, the building's oppressive atmosphere seemed to close around them.

The dark corridors of the psychiatric ward stretched before them, the air growing heavier with each step. The floor beneath them was worn, scuffed vinyl, softening the sound of their footsteps. The walls were cold and institutional, painted in a dull gray that matched the building's somber mood. The hum of fluorescent lights above added to the sterile, clinical feel of the place.

When they arrived at Dr. Conner's office, the heavy metal door creaked open with a groan, revealing a stark, functional room. Metal filing cabinets lined the walls, and a utilitarian desk occupied the center of the space. The faint scent of antiseptic mingled with the musty odor of old vinyl flooring.

Despite the presence of potted plants and framed art intended to add warmth, the atmosphere felt anything but comforting. The walls seemed to press in, amplifying the unease twisting in Karma's gut. She slumped in her chair, elbows on her knees, eyes on her shoes, fingers absentmindedly playing with the bandages around her wrists.

Vic stood beside her, his hand resting heavily on her shoulder, while Ophelia sat on the couch next to Antoinette, who wiped at her tear-streaked face. Dr. Conner stood behind her desk, calm and unreadable, observing the family in their chaotic state. "So, Karmela," Dr. Conner began, her tone neutral, "do you know why you're here at Helmbrook?"

A heavy silence hung over the room. Karma's eyes stayed glued to her sneakers, her fingers nervously tracing the frayed edges of the bandage on her wrist. Vic leaned in closer, his hand gripping her shoulder, giving her a gentle but firm shake. "Answer her, Karma," he said, his voice low and tight, trying to keep control.

Karma furrowed her brow, her voice a mere whisper.

"Yeah... I know what I did."

The tension in the room cracked as Vic's facial muscles tightened, his anger simmering just beneath the surface. Karma's dismissive tone and defiant words gnawed at him, pushing him to the brink of losing control.

"Your actions say otherwise, Karmela," he ground out, frustration lacing his voice. "Everything you do tells me you don't care if you live or die."

Karma's head snapped up, her fiery gaze locking onto his.

"Oh yeah?" she shot back, her voice thick with contempt.

"You think you know everything?"

"Yeah," Vic spat, his words dripping with venom. "It shows you don't give a damn about your family."

Her face twisted in fury. She flung her arms up in exasperation, her voice rising with frustration. "You sound stupid! You know that? Stupid!"

She paced forward, the anger radiating off her in waves. Her hands were still raised, almost daring something—anything—to challenge her. Her movements were sharp and restless, as if she could barely contain the rage boiling to the surface within her.

Every word she spat was laced with venom, each step charged with frustration.

The air between them felt heavy, suffocating, as if the room shook under the weight of their confrontation. Their emotions clashed, intense and raw, like a storm on the verge of breaking. Vic exhaled sharply, trying to steady himself, but the rising anger in his eyes betrayed his struggle to keep calm. Neither budged, their unspoken battle pressing on them, thick with resentment and pain.

"Stupid enough to put up with you and your nonsense," he finally said. However, his eyes softened, showing a glimmer of empathy.

"You're breaking your mother's heart."

"Oh, don't be so dramatic, Pa!" Karma sneered, her voice thick with contempt as she jabbed a finger toward him. "Go ahead, stick me in this place, then run home so Mom can give you a blow job and help you forget I exist."

Hahahahahaha. She let out a harsh, bitter laugh, her eyes blazing as she held his gaze, daring him to react. The room seemed to tighten around them, the tension palpable as her words cut through the air.

"Karma!" Vic shouted, his face red pissed right off, his voice trembling. "You're a disgusting child."

Ophelia rose swiftly, not sparing him a look. She gently took

Antoinette's hand, her touch gentle but firm.

"We're going to wait in the hall," she said, her voice soft as she led her youngest to the door. At the threshold, she stopped and turned back.

"We love you, Karmela," she added, her voice tender but thoroughly exhausted.

"Save it, Mom," Karma muttered, her cold eyes fixed on the floor. Her words cut, lingering like a slap that couldn't be taken back.

"Goddamn it," Vic muttered, his frustration brimming over, each word dripping with rage.

"Mr. Papadakis," Dr. Conner interjected calmly, "I've heard worse. Why don't you step outside for a minute? Take a breather." She gave him a look of quiet authority, offering him a moment to cool off before things escalated further. Vic stood there, the vein in his neck pulsing, his hands flexing and curling at his sides. For a moment, it seemed like he might explode, his hostility boiling over. With a sharp inhale, he turned on his heel and stormed out, slamming the door so hard that it echoed down the hall. He stammered past Ophelia and Antoinette, who were embracing on the bench in the hallway. Dr. Conner cleared her throat, turning to Karma with an assessing look.

"This must be hard for your family to watch you go through." "Whatever," Karma muttered, crossing her arms, her defenses rising like a wall.

"Do you feel detached from them?" She asked.

After pulling herself together, Karma muttered, "They don't get it," her voice low and gravelly, dripping with indifference. It had that familiar, rough "don't give a shit" tone, sharp at the edges, like a dare waiting for someone to challenge her. "You don't think anyone understands you?" Dr. Conner pushed gently.

Karma rolled her eyes. "Is this the part where you tell me I've got some hole inside I'm trying to fill? You're not good at this, you know that?"

"What do you think you need?" Dr. Conner asked.

"Nothing. I don't need help," Karma snapped. "I'm fine." Dr. Conner stood up, moving slowly around her desk before leaning against the front, arms crossed, her eyes locked on Karma.

"Forgive me," she began, her voice steady, "but taking a bunch of pills and cutting yourself in a bathtub doesn't exactly scream 'fine' to me."

Karma shifted uncomfortably in her chair. "I don't need to be here," she mumbled, her voice quieter and almost sad, as if she were trying to convince herself more than anyone else.

"This is a good place, Karma. We can help you here," Dr.

Conner said, her shoulders dropping as she relaxed. She felt reassured that her approach was starting to take effect, much to her delusion.

"I don't need help!" Karma shouted, jumping to her feet, her chair scraping harshly against the floor. "I don't want to be in a mental hospital."

Dr. Conner remained composed, leaning against her desk, hands folded in her lap. "This is a place to heal, to regroup, to find yourself," she said, her tone measured. Her eyes were fixed on Karma, trying to reach her.

Karma snickered and cracked a smile, her eyes squinting. "Find me? You're so full of shit," she snapped.

Dr. Conner didn't flinch. She stepped forward slightly, her voice calm. "Do you really think that's funny, Karma? The idea of people trying to heal?"

Her glare cut through Dr.Conner, her chest rising and falling with sharp breaths. "You're a joke," she spat, anger crackling between them.

There was a pause before Dr. Conner asked, "Are you on drugs right now, Karma?"

"I don't know, am I?" she replied.

Before the tension could deepen, a knock at the door broke the moment. Both women turned toward the sound, Ophelia's outline visible through the fogged glass.

"Mrs. Papadakis," Dr. Conner called out, "you can come in." The door clicked open, and Ophelia stepped inside, her face drawn tight with worry.

"Is everything okay?" she asked.

"Yes, everything is good; please sit."

She walked to the couch and sat just behind Karma, her posture tense.

"It's okay to feel this, Karma," Ophelia said gently. "You should feel something. It's normal."

Karma scoffed, turning to her mother. "I'm not normal. There's nothing normal about me." Her voice wavered, a hint of vulnerability slipping through. "I'm sorry I wasn't a normal child."

"Karma, we love you so much," Ophelia said, her voice thick with emotion. "We just want to help you."

"Stop talking like him!" Karma cut her off, her frustration mounting. "Say what you really feel, Mom! Speak for yourself! Say something real for once!"

Ophelia swallowed hard, her voice trembling. "Karmela... I know life is confusing, especially for you right now. But we can't watch you every second. You need someone there, at least until you don't want to hurt yourself anymore." She hesitated.

"We're going to go now."

Tears welled up in Karma's eyes, her voice cracking.

"Mommy, don't leave me here."

Dr. Conner stepped forward, but the raw emotion between mother and daughter filled the room.

"This is a safe place, Karma," Dr. Conner said again, her voice firm and confident.

Karma's frustration erupted. She shoved Dr. Conner with all her strength in a sudden burst of rage. The doctor stumbled backward, her arms flailing as she tried to regain her balance. She collided with the edge of the desk, her nose slamming into the corner with a sickening crack.

"Attendants! Attendants!" Dr. Conner cried out, clutching her nose as blood gushed out.

The door burst open, and two attendants rushed in, their faces blank with zero emotion. They moved swiftly, closing the distance between them and Karma, who was already defiantly flailing. Screams ripped from Karma's throat as she thrashed, fighting with everything she had against their grip. Ophelia stood frozen, eyes wide, trapped in helpless silence as chaos unfolded before her all over again.

"Sedate her!" Dr. Conner ordered, her voice edged with urgency. The attendants tightened their hold, struggling to control Karma as she kicked and flailed wildly, her shrieks piercing the room. "Mom! Help me! Mommy, don't let them take me!" Karma's desperate cries echoed through the hall, raw with panic and betrayal as the attendants dragged her away, still kicking and thrashing.

Ophelia's knees gave way, and she collapsed onto the couch, her hands instinctively flying to cover her face. Her body trembled with sobs, each breath jagged and unsteady, as the weight of the moment pressed down, suffocating her.

Dr. Conner wiped the blood from her face, pinching her nose with one hand as she slowly returned to her chair behind the desk. Her expression was a mix of exhaustion and empathy as she looked at Ophelia.

"She's in good hands now," Dr. Conner said softly, though her words felt hollow in the silence that followed. Ophelia's mind raced, swirling with the chaos of what had just happened. She wanted to believe Dr. Conner and cling to the hope that this place would help Karma find the peace she so desperately needed. But the gnawing fear in her chest refused to loosen its grip.

The door creaked open, and Vic stepped inside, his face pale and tense, burdened by the weight of it all. His eyes met Ophelia's, searching for any sign of reassurance. He found none.

Silently, he sank beside her, reaching for her hand, his grip firm while hers trembled.

"She'll be okay," Vic whispered, his voice thick, as though he needed to believe it himself.

Ophelia nodded, her voice barely audible. "She has to be," she replied, as though speaking louder might shatter the fragile hope she clung to.

Outside, the hallways of the psychiatric ward were eerily still. The only sounds were faint murmurs from the staff and the occasional creak of the old building settling into the early evening. A door clicked shut—a stark reminder of the isolation and the long road ahead for Karma and them. Therapy had never been part of their lives, let alone admitting their child to a mental hospital. It wasn't how they were raised; problems were handled quietly, privately. Now, they were stepping into unknown territory, the thought of leaving Karma here tearing at their hearts. Vic shifted uneasily, his leg bouncing, fingers tapping against his knee. Ophelia sat rigid, hands clenched in her lap, staring blankly at the floor, unable to focus on any one thought.

Dr. Conner finally broke the silence. "This is the beginning of a difficult journey," she said gently. "But it can lead to healing. We'll take it one step at a time and be with her every step of the way."

Vic squeezed her hand tighter, pulling her closer, drawing strength from their connection.

"We'll get through this," he said, his voice steady.

"Together, as a family."

Dennis

CHAPTER 3

THE SECRETS DENNIS KEEPS

Dennis was tall and slim, his face sunken and pale, like something pulled straight out of a nightmare. His hollow eyes gave him an eerie resemblance to the Night Stalker, Richard Ramirez. He moved down the hallway with a smugness in his stride, like he owned the place. Karma's heavy bag dangled from his hand, seemingly weightless, an afterthought in his grip.

The walls around him were chipped and crumbling, and the faint hum of flickering fluorescent lights buzzed overhead. When he reached the door on his left, he paused, glancing over his shoulder. Satisfied that no one was watching, he twisted the handle and slipped inside, the door clicking softly shut behind him as if the shadows swallowed him whole.

The door creaked on its hinges, revealing a dimly lit room where the weak light barely touched the corners. Eve lay curled on the bed, her frail form barely making an impression in the sheets, her eyes fixed on the yellowed pages of The Bell

Jar. The air in the room felt thick, as though it had been holding its breath, waiting for something to happen. The moment Dennis stepped inside, the weight pressed harder, like a storm ready to break. He stood at the door.

Eve lifted her head, her sunken, weary eyes meeting his briefly. The tension in the room thickened, hanging in the silence. Dennis broke it with a crooked, self-satisfied grin. "Got you a new roommate, Eve," he said, his voice too casual, almost mocking. He shut the door with a soft click, sealing them in.

Crossing the room with that same cocky swagger, he tossed Karma's bag onto the empty cot with a careless thud. The room, once Eve's solitary escape, felt tighter now, the walls creeping in and the shadows thickening around her. His fingers moved quickly, unzipping the bag and rummaging through Karma's things.

"What do we have here?" he murmured, pulling out her personal items individually. Eve kept her eyes on the book, but she wasn't reading—her heart pounded in her chest as she watched him from the corner of her eye.

His smile grew as he pulled out a pair of Karma's underwear. He held them to his face, inhaling deeply, then tucked them into his pocket with a sick sense of satisfaction. Zipping the bag back up, he turned his attention to Eve, his grin lingering like a dark stain.

Dennis approached the bed like a predator, closing in on

its prey. Eve didn't move, her fear tangible as he sat beside her. His touch was rough as his fingers traced every freckle and every mole—his on her skin.

She squeezed her eyes shut, forcing herself to endure the revolting sensation of his tongue sliding across her neck, bile rising in her throat. His rough fingers slid up her leg, scraping against her skin, each movement slow and calculated. Her t-shirt was pushed aside, his fingers finding the waistband of her underwear and sliding them down with unsettling ease. Eve lay frozen, body stiff, every breath shallow, as if the air had turned to poison. The weight of terror pinned her in place, each second stretching into an unbearable eternity.

Dennis moved with a sickening sense of ownership. His dry fingers clawed at her in a way that felt all too familiar, as though this violation was routine to him. With each flinch, each shudder of her discomfort, his grin grew wider, feeding off her helplessness. Eve's mind screamed, but her body remained still, trapped in the horror that suffocated her. Her fingers clenched the sheets, her body rigid beneath his assault. He forced her hand to his pants, his voice low and commanding.

"Rub it."

She obeyed without protest, her mind drifting somewhere far away as she went through the motions until he finished, leaving a wet make on his crotch.

Dennis stood, adjusting his pants with a smug smirk. He

glanced back at her, a twisted gleam in his eyes, then headed for the door, his shirt untucked to conceal the evidence of his crime and to cover up the wet spot. Without a word, he grasped the handle, pushed the door open, and slipped out, leaving a heavy silence as the door shut behind him.

A few seconds went by.

Eve lay trembling on the bed, her body betraying her as she sought release through shame-fueled relief, her knuckles moving in quick, desperate strokes.

Outside, Dennis ran a greasy hand through his thick, dark hair, slicking it back with a practiced motion. He spotted Nurse Bradie striding down the hall, her no-nonsense expression already warning him off, but his sly grin returned anyway.

"Hello, Nurse Bradie," he purred, sliding beside her with that overconfident swagger.

She barely spared him a glance.

"Hi, Dennis," she replied flatly, not breaking her stride. Her focus was on the night ahead, not him—he was just another irritation she had learned to tolerate.

He matched her pace; his presence stuck to her like chew-up gum, and she couldn't shake him.

"So, when are we going out?" he asked, his voice eager, eyes shining with a persistent intent. He leaned in closer, hoping to penetrate her wall of indifference.

Nurse Bradie let out a short, exasperated sigh.

"We're not, Dennis," she said firmly, still looking ahead, her steps steady. She had no time for his games and, indeed, no interest.

Dennis chuckled, undeterred.

"Come on, Bradie, it'd be fun. Dinner, drinks, I know a place."

She shot him a sharp look without missing a beat, her patience hanging by a thread.

"Not happening," she snapped, keeping her pace. "Find someone else for that."

But Dennis wasn't ready to give up, loving the challenge, the pushback.

"You'll come around," he muttered.

Nurse Bradie gave him a forced smile, her unnervingly white teeth making him flinch. He could almost imagine those teeth sinking into his skin.

"I told you, Dennis," she replied firmly, "I'm in a relationship."

As Nurse Bradie quickened her pace, Dennis's hand shot out, grabbing her wrist with an unexpected force that made her gasp. His grip was tight, almost bruising, and his breath brushed her ear, hot and menacing.

"Where do you think you're going?" he whispered, the threat slithering through his voice.

Her heart pounded in her chest, but she didn't freeze. Jerking her arm hard, she ripped free from his grasp, the suddenness of it causing her to stumble back.

"Far from you, Dennis," she spat, her voice quivering angrily. "As far as I can get."

Dennis stood there, his eyes locking onto her like a predator watching prey, dark and unblinking. His lips curled into that familiar, disgusting grin.

"Run all you want," he said, his voice low, laced with a venomous calm. "But you can't hide from me."

Bradie's steps faltered. She turned slowly, facing him head-on, the moment's weight sinking into her bones. Her hand slipped into her pocket, fingers wrapping around the cold metal of the small container she kept there for situations like this. She pulled it out, holding it between them. Her threat was clear and sharp.

"Don't be a creep, Dennis," she warned, her eyes narrowing.

"Or I'll spray you. And you don't want to find out how serious I am."

Dennis let out a low and sinister laugh, building from a quiet rumble to a mocking cackle that echoed around the room.

"Heh… heh… heh… Mwahaha!" It rolled out, twisted and dark, like he'd been waiting to unleash it all along.

Dennis stared at the mace, his grin faltering just enough to chill Nurse Bradie's spine. The flicker of uncertainty in his eyes didn't ease the tension—it made everything worse, twisting the moment into something even darker, more unnerving. His grin lingered in that twisted way, like he was weighing his options, pushing the boundaries to see how far he could go.

For a moment, the hallway stood still, with an awkward silence. The only sound was the dull hum of the overhead lights, flickering as if they, too, were holding their breath. Nurse Bradie's hand tightened around the mace. She didn't say another word and didn't need to. The air between them crackled, frozen in the standoff, until she stepped back, breaking the tension.

Dennis didn't follow her; he just watched her go, and that unsettling grin never entirely left his face. With each step she took down the dim hallway, her heart slowly began to steady, but the significance of his gaze lingered heavily on her back.

The door at the end of the hall closed behind her.

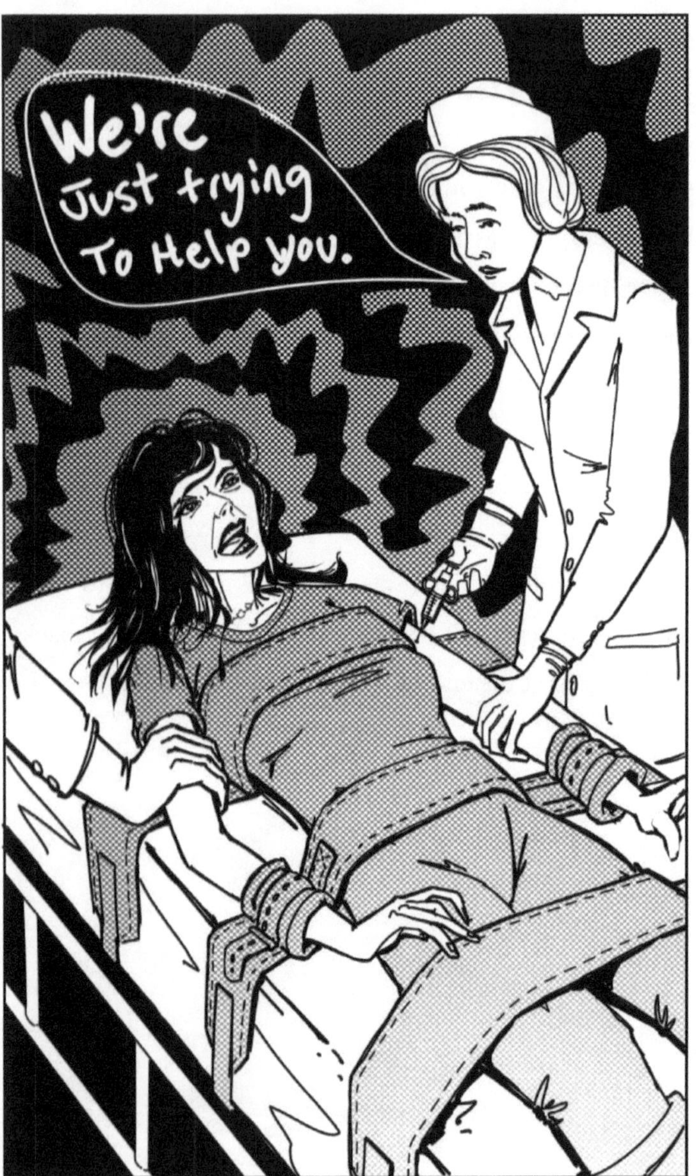

We're just trying to Help you.

CHAPTER 4

UNDER THE INFLUENCE

"Let go of me!" Karma yelled, her voice echoing down the sterile corridor and bouncing off the walls. Her legs kicked frantically, arms flailing as the attendants gripped her tightly by the biceps and wrists, dragging her forward.

"We're just trying to help you." one of the attendants spat, tightening his grip as Karma thrashed harder.

"Fuck you, man! I don't belong here!" she screamed, her voice breaking with desperation, every muscle in her body straining against their hold.

The cold, sterile hallway stretched out with metal doors, standing like silent soldiers. Behind a few, Coco, Louise, and Carmen watched through narrow cracks, their faces tight with unease.

Coco watched as Karma fought against the attendants like a wild animal. Louise shook her head.

Carmen leaned in closer, her voice barely a murmur, "She's

like the last one." she said, whatever that meant.

Karma's screams echoed down the hallway, "I don't belong here!" But the way the attendants pinned her down said otherwise.

"I want to be free!" Karma's voice cracked with desperation, her struggles becoming more frantic.

Fluorescent lights hummed overhead, casting a cold, clinical glow on the scene. Violet and Selena appeared from the TV room, drawn by the noise. At the far end of the hallway, Eve stood alone by the door—thin, meek, her short blonde hair catching the light. She watched as Karma was dragged closer.

"This is your new roommate, Eve," one of the more prominent attendants said as they passed her.

They hauled Karma into a nearby exam room, her voice growing hoarse with protest.

"I'm not crazy! Let me go!" Karma yelled, her words laced with fury, her eyes flashing with increased panic as things went from bad to worse. The attendants remained firm, guiding her inside and closing the door as Karma's voice cracked with rage.

"I'm not crazy! Let me go!" Her eyes were wild with frantic desperation, panic swirling as she struggled against their grip. "This is a mistake! You can't keep me here!"

The room was bathed in soft, muted light, its walls painted in pale blues and greens, colors meant to calm. But the air told a different story. The sharp bite of antiseptic lingered, barely masked by a faint hint of lavender from an air freshener. The cold, sterile smell of the hospital clung to every surface, impossible to escape.

The two attendants stood by the metal-framed bed, watching Karma with wary eyes as she struggled against the straps that now bound her. Nurse Bradie approached, her expression gentle but firm, a syringe in hand.

"It's okay, darling," Nurse Bradie said as she administered the injection, her voice a soothing murmur.

Karma's response was immediate—a piercing scream that cut through the room like a blade, shaking with raw anger.

"No! Get off me!" she cried, thrashing against the restraints, her voice reverberating off the walls and drowning out the low hum of the fluorescent lights.

"We're just trying to help you, Karma," Nurse Bradie repeated, though her words were lost beneath Karma's fierce cries.

"Fuck you, fuck all of you! Stop saying you're trying to help me," Karma spat, staring up at the harsh light as her vision blurred, the tears turning into shimmering diamonds that hung in the air, distorting everything around her.

The nurse and attendants exchanged a look, all too familiar with this routine. They'd seen it countless times—the initial struggle, the wild desperation, and the slow fade as the drugs kicked in.

Karma's thrashing slowed, her limbs growing heavy as the

sedative seeped into her system. Her body gave up the fight, trembling one last time before going still. Moments later, she was out, slipping into unconsciousness as the hallway returned to its cold, sterile quiet.

In a nearby room, Eve sat on her hard bed, a copy of the book The Bell Jar open in her lap. A faint, unpleasant odor lingered in the air, making the room feel smaller. The click of the door latch cut through the silence, flooding the room with light as the door swung open.

Two attendants entered, pushing a gurney with Karma's limp body strapped to it. They moved with methodical efficiency, lifting her onto the empty bed. Once they unstrapped her wrists and positioned her on the stiff sheets, they glanced briefly at Eve, who sat curled on the other bed, watching them intently.

Karma stirred, her movements sluggish, weighed down by exhaustion. Her eyelids fluttered, too heavy to fully open, and a dull ache radiated from her stiff neck. Drool collected at the corner of her mouth, trickling down her chin as her head sank deeper into the pillow. Her eyes were unfocused and glassy.

Eve stared at her new roommate, her expression timid and guarded. She leaned over, stood, and placed the styrofoam cup of lukewarm tap water on the small side table beside Karma's bed. The cup's rim was faintly marked with teeth imprints, a sign of its repeated use.

She hesitated, her eyes briefly locking with Karma's before

quickly darting away, uncomfortable under the crushing awkwardness of the moment.

Then, with an unexpected surge of defiance, Karma snapped her knees up, knocking the cup to the floor. Water splashed across the plastic floor, spreading in jagged lines, breaking the sterile silence of the room.

Eve flinched, her hands trembling as she watched the water spread across the floor.

Her heart fluttered, but she said nothing, simply turning away. A mix of emotions stirred inside, but she pushed them down, like always. Moving back to her bed, she curled up, pulling her book close, gripping the pages more for comfort than reading. The hard candy in her mouth offered a slight, familiar distraction, but it did little to calm her nerves.

"Lights out," a stern voice echoed down the hallway.

Eve sat in the shadows, her small frame almost swallowed by the darkness. She stared at Karma, whose eyes were closed, a soft snore escaping her partially opened mouth as she slept off the sedatives.

ZZZZZZZZ
psych ward

CHAPTER 5

NOT IN KANSAS ANYMORE

The next day, the ward jolted to life with its usual chaos. Buzzzzzzzzz. The bell rang, sharp and grating, cutting through the muffled voices and shuffling feet like a blade. It was an obnoxious, unforgiving sound that shattered whatever thin layer of calm the morning had tried to hold onto and snapped everyone into the ward's relentless routine.

Karma jerked awake, her body slow and sluggish from the meds that had kept her under all night. She blinked against the pale light filtering through the window, squinting as her groggy mind struggled to shake off the fog. Every limb felt heavy like she was weighed down by something unseen, making even the slightest movement a struggle.

"Shut up!" she yelled at the alarm, her voice hoarse and thick with exhaustion. The fluorescent lights cast a dull, sickly greenish tint across the room, making everything feel cold and washed out. She blinked hard, her eyes adjusting, and with a sinking feeling, it all came rushing back—where she was and what she couldn't escape.

"Fuckin' hell," she mumbled under her breath, wiping the sticky drool from the corner of her mouth. She took a deep breath, trying to shake off the lingering grogginess. Her throat was dry, the taste of sleep still clinging to her tongue. As she sat there, trying to gather her thoughts, it felt like her mind was stuck in quicksand—slow, heavy, and impossible to pull free from.

The door swung open, making Karma jump. Nurse Stone strode in, her steps quick and precise. Tall and thin, with a stern, no-nonsense expression, she looked as severe as the air she carried. Middle-aged and sharp as ever, she moved with the efficiency from years of experience in this job. Her eyes swept over the room coldly, revealing nothing of her thoughts.

"Last call for breakfast," she announced, her voice cutting through the haze. She leaned over Karma, tugging at the sheets before flicking on a penlight and checking her pupils. "Stick out your tongue and say 'ahh,'" she instructed, her tone cold and clinical. Karma hesitated, feeling the sharp smell of disinfectant cling to her senses. She grimaced as Nurse Stone pried open her mouth, the intrusion feeling incredibly invasive and so early in the morning.

"Good morning to you, too," Karma mumbled sarcastically, but Nurse Stone didn't even acknowledge her. She continued the exam, her movements mechanical as if she'd done this a thousand times before. After a quick once-over, Nurse Stone straightened up.

Without a word, she turned and walked toward the door.

"Hurry up, or you'll miss breakfast," she called over her shoulder, not bothering to look back.

"Is there coffee?" Karma asked, still buried in sweat-stained sheets.

"If you hurry," Nurse Stone replied, clapping her hands before disappearing through the door and leaving it slightly ajar.

The female wing of the institution was tucked away on the outskirts of the hospital, a dilapidated building reserved for the most challenging patients. It was brutally underfunded, starkly contrasting to the main hospital a few buildings over. The once-bright walls were now dull and peeling, giving the place a ghostly, abandoned look. The air was heavy with a musty odor that clung to the linens and hung in the dimly lit hallways like a stale fog.

Two girls were locked in a fierce argument in the TV room, their voices cutting through the uneasy silence. Elsewhere, patients wandered the ward, pacing with nervous energy. A girl slept in the corner, blissfully unaware of the tension around her, the light from the barred windows casting a soft glow on her form.

The phone rang continuously at the nurse's station, contributing to the chaos of the morning. The sound of footsteps echoed on the vinyl floors while distant murmurs from the staff and the shuffle of feet combined into an unsettling hum that filled the air.

Karma made her way to the cafeteria, greeted by the acrid scent of burnt coffee from the self-serve station. The staff had been trained to create a comforting environment, but it was a half-hearted effort. The large, barred windows let in the cool morning light, diffused by a cloudy sky, revealing the hospital garden outside. This untamed, overgrown mess mirrored the neglect inside the building.

She shuffled over to the coffee percolator, hoping for a caffeine hit, only to find a sign that read, "Decaf."

"God damn it," she growled, grabbing a chipped mug.

She hesitated momentarily before pouring herself a cup of the sad, watery coffee left at the bottom of the pot. Grabbing a stale bagel, she scanned the pitiful breakfast spread before her: lumpy oatmeal, tin cups of mushy fruit salad, powdery scrambled eggs, and plain yogurt that looked like it had been sitting out too long. The whole table felt like an afterthought. Open jars of jam and cheap peanut butter sat next to a misshapen lump of butter on a chipped plate, with a few dull knives awkwardly sticking out. It was a bleak sight, the kind of meal that made you lose your appetite before the first bite.

The cafeteria could have been a more organized mess, with staff lazily wiping down the counters. Plates of half-eaten fruit salad and spoiled yogurt were cleared away, the clatter of utensils scraping against trays, grated on Karma's nerves. The room felt stale, and the noise only added to her irritation.

She picked a vacant seat by the window, seeking peace, but the heavy smells of reheated food and harsh cleaning products made her stomach churn.

"You're such a bitch!" Selena's voice cut through the uneasy calm of the room, her glare fixed on Violet, who sat silently under the assault.

"I can't believe you'd do something so stupid!" Selena's voice escalated, her fury unmistakable. Her eyes blazed as she gestured wildly, almost daring Violet to respond.

Carmen slid into the seat across from Karma with a sudden thud, the motion jarring enough to pull Karma's attention for a split second.

"Hey, beautiful person," Carmen said, her voice clear and playful. Karma tensed, unfamiliar with the girl but immediately unsettled. The way Carmen moved felt like an unpredictable energy radiated from her. Then, a strange clicking sound started—a steady, rhythmic noise from Carmen's jaw that bothered Karma almost instantly. When Carmen suddenly screamed, the sharp noise made Karma flinch. Her grip tightened on the table's edge, knuckling white, as her heart raced. She stared straight ahead, trying to keep calm, but the unease prickled at her skin.

Karma stood up, ready to leave, tuning out the escalating commotion behind her. Selena's tirade had grown louder, her voice now aimed at anyone listening.

"You don't know what you're talking about!" Violet stammered, her voice shaky and desperate.

"You're drowning in denial, Violet! Reality check!" Selena snapped back, her neck craning forward as she gestured dramatically, her frustration spilling over in exaggerated motions.

Just as Karma reached the door, ready to slip out, Nurse Stone appeared in front of her, blocking her path with that familiar. . . I'm a fucking bitch attitude.

"No food or drink outside the cafeteria," Nurse Stone stated, her tone flat and cold, blocking Karma's path like an immovable wall.

Karma didn't look at her.

"I saw people with cups out there," she shot back, her voice defiant.

"They shouldn't have," Stone snapped, her voice cutting through the air with a sharp edge.

Karma's eyes finally locked with Nurse Stone's, filled with defiance. She stuffed the entire bagel into her mouth, never breaking eye contact. Chewing exaggeratedly, she tipped her coffee cup to the side of her mouth. The liquid poured out, dribbling messily down her chin and splattering onto her shirt.

Not giving a fuck, she let the moment out.

Then, with a toss, she hurled the rest of the bagel and coffee into the trash, wiping her chin with the back of her hand. Karma sauntered past Nurse Stone, every step dripping with a single and unmistakable message: Fuck Off.

ME!
Who took !
MY SMOKES?
SMOKES
Bridget

CHAPTER 6

SMOKE AND ASH

Karma dragged herself into the room, shoulders slumped, her whole body radiating indifference. The door hit the wall with a dull thud, but she barely noticed. Her eyes moved anxiously, scanning the drab, sterile walls, the same suffocating atmosphere she had been trying to escape since the moment she arrived.

Every step she took felt heavy as if she were ready to snap at the slightest push. This place, these people—they were starting to wear her down. She'd been there less than twenty-four hours, and the boredom was killing her, but she wasn't about to let it show. Not yet.

Her lean frame buzzed with restless energy, and her black hair spilled in tangled waves around her shoulders. Spotting an empty chair by the TV, Karma made her way over and sank into the worn, oversized brown seat.

The chair groaned under her weight, its fabric frayed and

faded from years of use. Her sharp, dark eyes flicked around the room, taking in every corner before finally settling on the television. Her mind began to drift, thoughts blurring under the weight of exhaustion and the haze of meds coursing through her.

Absentmindedly, her fingers found the bandages on her wrist, twisting and tugging at them in a nervous, rhythmic motion.

Time blurred. Seconds stretched into minutes, minutes into hours. The noise of the ward—the droning TV, distant voices, and the clatter of utensils from the cafeteria—faded into the thick haze, pulling her deeper into herself. Colors dulled, and the edges of the room blurred. Karma sank into the chair, trying to disconnect from the moment entirely. But a prickling sensation crept up her spine—someone was watching her.

She turned and found Bridget staring, her expression distant and unnerving. Karma raised an eyebrow, breaking the silence.

"Got a staring problem?" she asked, her voice rough. Her eyes shifted to the pack of cigarettes resting on the armrest beside Bridget, and her tone lightened.

"Can I have a smoke?"

Bridget had yet to respond. She sat like a statue, her face blank and her mind far away. The silence stretched, and frustration floated to the surface in Karma. She leaned forward, tapping her fingers on the table with growing impatience.

"Hey," Karma said, snapping her fingers in front of Bridget's face.

"Can I get a smoke? Hello?" Her voice sharpened as she grew louder.

Bridget barely moved her only response a lazy shrug as her gaze drifted to the pack of cigarettes before her.

"What, you don't talk?" Karma sighed, her patience running thin. She stood and walked over, her shadow casting over Bridget as she loomed above. Finally, Bridget's eyes lifted, meeting Karma's with a slow, unsettling smile that never quite reached her eyes.

Without hesitation, Karma reached for the pack, fingers brushing against the lone cigarette flipped upside down—a smoker's superstition for luck. She smirked and, naturally, took that one.

The lighter snapped open with a soft click, followed by the quiet hiss of flame. The cigarette crackled to life, the sharp scent of burning tobacco quickly filling the air. Karma drew in a deep breath, the smoke curling into her lungs, the raw burn in her throat strangely soothing. As she exhaled, a thin stream of smoke floated lazily into the room, and for a brief moment, she let herself sink into the calm.

"Thanks," Karma muttered sarcastically and flopped back into her chair, blowing smoke rings in Bridget's direction.

Bridget clapped her hands, entertained as the rings dissolved in the air. Karma took another drag, her eyes flicking back to Bridget.

"What's your name?" she asked, the words curling out with the smoke. When Bridget didn't answer, Karma's tone hardened. "I'm Karma. What's your name?" she repeated, pointing directly at her.

Bridget's hands fumbled through the deep pockets of her baggy institutional clothes—faded gray sweats and a loose, oversized shirt draped over her like a blanket. The fabric, worn soft from endless washes, made her almost disappear into the sterile, lifeless room. After a moment, her fingers found a crumpled scrap of an index card. She pulled it out, the edges bent and frayed from being handled too many times.

She handed it over to Karma, who unfolded it slowly, the paper crackling in her hands. Squinting at the uneven scrawl, Karma read aloud, "Bridget." Her eyes looked up from the card, meeting Bridget's, then looking away.

"Your name's Bridget," she said, her voice flat but curious. Karma leaned back in the chair, her eyes fixed on Bridget, sizing her up under the harsh fluorescent light. With a quick jerk of her neck, Karma leaned back, tapping the ash from her cigarette onto the floor without a second thought. Bridget nodded, her eyes lighting up momentarily like some switch had flipped inside her.

Louise barreled through the door, her steps heavy and

loud, shaking the floor beneath her. Without slowing down, she stormed into the room, a sneer twisting her face, eyes burning with irritation. The air tensed as the room fell silent, everyone sensing the shift. Louise was in one of her moods, and nothing good was coming.

"Where are my smokes?" Louise growled, marching over to Bridget's chair. She snatched the cigarette pack off the armrest and glared down at Bridget, who smiled back, unbothered.

"Fuck you, retard girl," Louise said to her, flipping open the pack and counting the cigarettes. She turned to leave but stopped midway. She whirled back to Bridget.

"Yo!" she barked. "Don't smile at me. Did you take one of my cigarettes?" Louise stomped toward her, grabbing Bridget's shoulders and shaking her. Bridget's blank expression didn't change, her eyes reflecting only confusion.

"Did you take my cigarettes?" Louise shouted again, inches from Bridget's face.

Karma stood, her voice calm but firm. "I took your smoke; leave her alone. Beeeeaaach."

Louise's anger flared in an instant. She shoved Bridget, sending her sprawling onto the couch, then turned, locking her full attention on Karma. Karma didn't budge. She stared right back and flipped Louise off, the cigarette butt still smoldering between her fingers.

Without warning, Louise lunged. Her fist connected with

Karma's nose, and they both crashed to the floor, grappling wildly. Blood smeared across Karma's face as she fought back.

Bridget watched silently from the corner, clapping and cheering them on without uttering a word, her mute presence amplifying the chaos.

Two male orderlies rushed in, pulling the girls apart, but the scuffle didn't end there. Two more attendants hurried in, armed with straps and straight jackets. Karma and Louise were quickly restrained the rough fabric of the jackets constricting around them.

Karma spotted Bridget off to the side, sitting quietly with her usual goofy smile and utterly unfazed by the mayhem. Her tongue stuck out slightly like she was watching a circus, oblivious—or maybe just indifferent—to how intense things had become.

Karma was dragged out, blood trickling from her nose and mouth. She fought against the orderlies, her breath coming in harsh breaths.

She glanced over her shoulder at Bridget, her face blank, but something flickered in her eyes before the door slammed shut behind her.

Louise was still yelling, her voice sharp and wild with rage as she thrashed against the orderlies.

"Get your hands off me! You fuckin' pigs! I'll kill you!" she spat, kicking and swinging at anything within reach.

"Let go! Do you think you're tough? I'll rip your damn

heads off!" She bucked violently, her fury echoing down the hall as they dragged her away. "Let go of me, you fuckers!"

The chaos slowly faded, leaving the room in heavy silence, broken only by the low hum of the TV playing some forgotten infomercial in the background. The droning voice echoed off the walls, filling the space where the shouting had been moments before.

CHAPTER 7

KILL ME PLEASE

The door burst open with a sharp crack, echoing through the room as the attendants shoved Karma inside. She fought against them, thrashing as much as the straitjacket allowed. The thick fabric crushed her chest, every breath a struggle, her lungs burning under the suffocating pressure. She gasped, chest heaving, desperate for air as the attendants wrestled her forward, barely containing her wild, jerking movements.

"Fuck, shit, bitch!" she screamed, the words muffled by the jacket. She bit down on the stiff collar, tasting the bitter, musty fabric. Stumbling backward, she collapsed onto the cot, landing face down, her legs twisted awkwardly beneath her. Her heart hammered, and her breathing grew shallow, a knot tightening in her throat as she spiraled, emotions slipping out of control.

Time became meaningless. Only a faint trickle of light slipped through the narrow window, barely enough to cast the faintest shadow on the floor. The room stayed cloaked in a dim, oppressive gray, unchanged as the hours passed. The muffled sounds of distant voices and footsteps in the hallway drifted in and out, lost in the thick quiet that filled the space.

Karma's breathing slowed, her chest rising and falling steadily. Soft, wheezing snores slipped through her parted lips and congested nose, breaking the silence. Outside, life went on, but in that room, time felt frozen, as if it had left her behind. Hours drifted by unnoticed, the muted sounds of the ward fading into the background as she lay wrapped in a restless, uneasy sleep.

Suddenly, Karma's eyes snapped open, a sharp gasp escaping her lips as she jolted awake, her arms twitching involuntarily. The straitjacket was gone, but the suffocating tightness lingered in her chest, the medication's dull grip still heavy in her veins. Disoriented, she sat up, her heart racing as she tried to shake off the fog clinging to her mind.

Across the room, Eve sat on her bed, bathed in the soft glow of a small lamp. The light cast long shadows over her sharp features as she pored over *The Bell Jar*, seemingly absorbed in the pages. But Karma knew Eve had noticed her wake—there was a tension in the air, a quiet expectation as if Eve was waiting for her to say something.

Karma's mind raced, trying to piece together where she was. The eerie stillness of the room only heightened her unease, making her more restless by the second. She shifted on the bed, her movements sluggish, until she perched on the edge of the mattress. The cotton swabs stuffed in her nose still blocked the last traces of blood from the fight, and her hair clung in tangled strands to her sweaty face. Her eyes were swollen, and the bridge of her nose throbbed, still tender from the punch.

Blinking to clear her vision, she felt the room spin faintly around her.

"Hi, I'm Eve," she finally said, glancing up from her book.

"Good for you," Karma replied, her expression hardening as she sat up straighter. She studied Eve, eyes narrowed and unreadable, the air between them thick with silence. Karma fixed her gaze on Eve, observing every slight movement as if waiting for something to change.

"What's your name?" Eve asked, breaking the awkward tension.

Karma scoffed. "What does it matter?" she shot back casually.

Without a word, Eve reached under her mattress and pulled out a half-melted chocolate bar, holding it out. Karma hesitated but eventually took it, unwrapping it slowly. She bit into the chocolate, feeling her shoulders relax a little.

"Karma," she finally said.

Eve grinned. "Cool name."

Karma smirked, then casually flipped her off. "You into girls? 'Cause I'm not interested."

Eve shrugged without missing a beat. "I'm not into

anything."

Karma paused mid-bite, raising an eyebrow. "What the hell does that mean?"

"I'm asexual," Eve replied, snapping her book shut.

Karma chewed, her face skeptical. "So… you're not a lesbo?" Eve shrugged again. "I like guys and girls… or sometimes no one at all. Depends on the day."

Karma shook her head. "I don't think you've got that right."

"Yeah, I do," Eve insisted.

Karma chuckled softly. "Nah. Asexual means you don't like anyone, you fool. . . Like, at all."

Eve thought for a second.

"Really? Huh… I'm not so sure about that."

"I am. You're bi, maybe even tri," Karma shot back, pulling her knees to her chest and taking another bite of chocolate. Her thoughts swirled, both confused and amused. She couldn't quite figure Eve out—this girl who seemed detached yet oddly sure of herself in the weirdest way.

Karma was always ready for a fight, always prepared to push people away before they could push her. But Eve wasn't biting.

And that annoyed her.

"Isn't it against the rules to have chocolate?" Karma asked, chewing the last piece of the candy bar.

Eve smiled slyly, her pencil-thin legs dangling off the cot's edge. "For the right favor, you can get anything in here." Karma glanced around the room. "I need a phone. You got one of those under there?" She nodded toward Eve's mattress.

"Nope," Eve replied, stretching out on her bed, completely unbothered.

Karma leaned back, eyes fixed on the wooden headboard.

"Well then, what good are you?"

Her gaze froze as she noticed something scratched into the wood: **PLEASE KILL ME**. Her breath caught for a second but didn't let it show.

"What about drugs?" Karma asked, her eyes still locked on the words.

Eve stood, lifting her mattress again and pulling out a crumpled brown paper bag. She unrolled it and dropped a small pillbox into her palm. Karma's eyes lit up as Eve stepped closer, opening the box.

"What are they?" Karma asked, leaning forward, her pulse quickening.

"The round ones are Gravol—for motion sickness," Eve said, rattling the box. "Take like five, and you'll start hallucinating."

Karma wrinkled her nose. "No thanks. What about the others?"

"The tiny blue ones make you sleepy. The white ones with the line down the middle? Those are speedy. They'll give you a good buzz."

Karma's eyes dilated with interest. "I can get down with that."

Eve handed her two of the blue pills. "Take both. They're not strong. Keep the white one for when you need to perk up." Without hesitation, Karma popped the pills into her mouth, swallowing them dry, ignoring the styrofoam cup of water Eve held out. She leaned back, waiting for the numbing effects to kick in.

Eve stashed the pills back under the mattress and sat on her bed, watching her. "What happened to your wrists?" she asked, nodding toward the bandages peeking from Karma's sleeves. Karma's face darkened. "What do you think?" she snapped, her tone sharp.

"Um, I figured—" Eve stammered.

"I had an accident with a razor," Karma interrupted, her words cold and cutting.

Eve went quiet, retreating into herself as she pulled her knees to her chest. The atmosphere shifted, the tension thickening like a weight between them.

"Is that why you're here?" Eve asked softly, her voice barely above a whisper.

Karma looked away momentarily, then back at Eve, her expression unreadable. "I guess," she muttered, shrugging as she flipped her long, tangled black hair.

"Your hair is so thick and black," Eve said, reaching out like she might touch it.

Karma jerked back, laughing nervously. "Hey, just friends, alright? Don't touch me."

Eve smiled sheepishly, brushing her strawberry-blonde bangs out of her face. "I was just saying... I wish I had better hair."Karma's hardened expression softened a little, the corners of her lips twitching into a faint smile.

"Relax. I'm just joking with you," she said, her tone lighter, a trace of warmth slipping through. The stiffness in her shoulders eased as she let out a quiet breath, and the tension between them slowly faded.

"We're all in the same boat here," Eve muttered, her voice trailing off like she was trying to convince herself more than Karma.

Karma didn't respond immediately, her eyes lingering on Eve, studying her. A flicker of mistrust lingered in Karma's gaze, wariness still clinging. After a moment, she sighed, the weight settling deep in her chest.

"Yeah, I guess," she finally said, her voice quiet but strained. She glanced away, her eyes hardening with resolve. "But I'm getting the fuck out of here. I can promise you that."

The room fell silent. Eve didn't dare push back. Karma's words hung in the air, heavy with determination, the promise that didn't need to be repeated.

Lets take some pics.
No

CHAPTER 8

SINS OF SURVIVAL

The Valium hit, dulling her senses and blurring the world's edges. It was more potent than Karma had expected, dragging her into a fog where everything felt distant like she was floating but trapped in her body. The reality of being stuck in the institute smeared across her mind like she was stuck in a never-ending bad 90s sitcom rerun. Each day bled into the next—an endless loop of suffocating routine that gnawed at her sanity. The tension in the air pressed down, making it hard to breathe; every moment stretched so thin it felt ready to snap. There was no escape, just the same monotonous grind pulling her deeper into its grip.

She spent most of her time alone, oddly comforted by the quiet and strange presence of her little roommate, Eve. As day turned to night, the atmosphere in the hospital shifted. The air inside was always stale—like it had been trapped for decades.

The door creaked open slowly, the sound breaking the

silence. A thin beam of light slipped into the room, stretching across the floor, dark shapes twisting and curling as they moved closer. Dennis stepped inside, his figure outlined against the harsh hallway light. His presence seemed to swallow the weak glimmer, an unsettling force that warped the space around him. His smile never reached his eyes, and a coldness in his gaze sent a quiet chill through the air. His smooth, low voice could be disarming, but something darker simmered beneath it, feeding on control.

Outside, the moonlight fought to break through the dense trees surrounding the institution, casting an eerie, almost otherworldly glow over the grounds. The hospital seemed to fold in on itself, a forgotten relic wrapped in silence and shadow, untouched by the world beyond.

Security was loose, and the place felt abandoned at night—most of the night crew just hung around, barely paying attention, letting the hours drift by.

Nurse Stone, cigarette dangling from her fingers, strode from the building to her beat-up Chevy. She yanked the door open, slid inside, and turned the key. The engine sputtered to life, coughing before settling into a low rumble. After letting it idle for a moment, she drove off into the fog, her taillights slowly swallowed by the mist.

As usual, Eve sat cross-legged on her bed, engrossed in her book. The meds she'd given Karma and the nurse's nightly dose created a potent cocktail. Karma snored softly, her upper lip twitching, body limp and heavy, trapped in the thick haze of the drugs.

The door creaked open, breaking the silence. A thin beam of light slipped into the room, crawling across the floor like a twisted finger, inching closer.

Dennis stepped inside, his figure stark against the harsh hallway light. Something magnetic about him drew attention—the way his smile never quite reached his eyes and the unsettling coldness in his gaze. His smooth and low voice could be disarming, but beneath it lurked something darker, something dangerous. Dennis thrived on control. His ability to manipulate with subtle gestures and carefully chosen words made him unpredictable, and that made him even more dangerous.

He approached Eve, a sleazy grin creeping onto his face as he handed her a small, plastic-wrapped object. Eve accepted it with a faint smirk, her lips curling just enough to hint at something hidden. Her eyes glinted in the shadowed light, a mix of innocence and something darker, unreadable, making the moment both playful and unsettling. Dennis's attention shifted to Karma. Casually, he slipped a hand into his pocket and pulled out a battered flip phone—an old Motorola with a scratched screen and chipped edges. He flipped it open with a quiet snap, the weak glow casting a dull light on his face. After fiddling with the buttons momentarily, his gaze locked on Karma's motionless body, the phone resting loosely in his hand, almost forgotten as he watched her.

Without hesitation, he yanked the blanket down, exposing her, and began snapping pictures with the phone's camera, his fingers moving quickly across the buttons.

As he turned to Eve, his grin stretched wide, revealing a set of yellow-brownish, crooked teeth that resembled baked beans, uneven and grotesque.

"Come here. Hurry up," he hissed, his voice filled with menace, gesturing towards the bed where Karma lay.

Eve hesitated, standing there in nothing but an oversized white shirt and skimpy panties. She shifted uncomfortably, her bare feet cold against the floor, feeling the weight of his gaze crawling over her. Dennis's grin deepened, and his eyes gleamed with something far darker than curiosity. He nodded toward the bed again, his unspoken command lingering.

"Get next to her," he repeated, his words sharp and deliberate, leaving no room for defiance.

Eve obediently climbed onto the bed beside Karma, positioning herself awkwardly close to her sedated roommate.

"Closer," Dennis whispered, snapping more pictures. "And be sexy."

Eve slid over, her hand hovering just above Karma's chest before resting on her breasts, rubbing them lightly. She stuck out her tongue dangerously close to Karma's closed lips.

"Hold that," Dennis instructed, moving in closer. The camera flashed as he captured the scene. His breath came in short, eager like a dog panting.

"Slide her shirt up... I want to see her legs and ass," he ordered, his eyes gleaming with sick anticipation.

Eve hesitated, her body stiff as she followed his instructions mechanically. Dennis grinned, switched the phone to video mode, and hit record. The screen flickered to life, but the video was pixelated, the quality grainy and distorted. Suddenly, a sharp clang echoed from the hallway—metal hitting the vinyl floor with a loud crash. The sound shattered the quiet of the hospital wing, reverberating through the empty corridors. Dennis and Eve froze, their bodies tense, caught off guard by the sudden noise.

Dennis's eyes darted to Karma, who remained motionless on the bed, still deep in her drug-induced sleep. He put a finger to his lips, signaling Eve to stay quiet, then gently pushed her off the bed. He quickly pulled the sheet back over Karma's body, glancing toward the door cautiously. The room fell into an uneasy silence, the distant clang reverberating in their minds. Outside the door, the hospital ward was thick with a dark calm that often settled in after lights out. The meds gave the patients a false sense of calm, a temporary blanket over the chaos simmering beneath the surface. But Dennis knew it wouldn't last; it never did. The demons always found a way to break through.

Memories
coco
Patient: Violet
DOB:1974 Age:17 Sex:F
Psychiatric ward

CHAPTER 9

SELENA'S WHISPER

Karma's lip throbbed, swollen from the punch Louise had thrown. Every slight movement sent a sharp sting through the cut, the skin tight and sore. The dull ache lingered, pulsing in time with her heartbeat. Her nose ached, bruised from the punch, and the dark circles under her bloodshot eyes only added to the exhaustion weighing her down. Slumped in the chair, legs sprawled, she stared blankly at the sterile white walls. It felt like she was trapped in some twisted, sanitized prison—everything too clean, too quiet. But the pain was real, and deep down, Karma couldn't shake the feeling that she was stuck.

Around her, the other girls sat in a circle, their chatter rattling like bones in a blender—loud and pointless.

"They need to let us out more," Violet muttered, her eyes glued to the barred windows as if staring long enough would set her free. "I've been stuck in here for weeks. Haven't seen the outside for more than an hour."

"Wow, shocker. That's what happens when you're crazy," Selena shot back with a dry laugh, not glancing up from her nails. "And by the way, you were out in the yard like yesterday. Stop acting like such a victim."

A weak, mean-spirited chuckle rippled through the group.

Violet's head snapped up, eyes blazing with anger.

"Don't call me that," she spat, her fists tightening until her knuckles turned white.

"Or what?" Selena leaned forward, her smirk widening. "You gonna cry about it?"

Karma sank deeper into her chair, rolling her eyes so hard she thought they might get stuck. The whole scene was pathetic—petty, childish arguing over nothing. It made her want to block it all out, shutting off from the nonsense around her. She stared at the ceiling, letting her mind wander, drifting far from the pointless drama unfolding before her.

"What the hell are you smiling at?" Selena snapped, her sharp tone cutting through the noise like a knife.

Karma let out a loud, exaggerated sigh, her eyes still fixed on the ceiling. "Oh, nothing," she drawled. "Just enjoying the show—watching you all act like a bunch of little bitches who didn't get their beauty sleep."

Selena's eyes narrowed, and her fists flexed.

"You got something to say, new girl?"

Karma glanced over, meeting Selena's glare with bored indifference.

"I think I already said it, didn't I?"

She lazily looked around the room, her expression dripping with sarcasm, mocking Selena's attempt at being tough.

"You think you're tough, huh?"

Selena stood up, tension spiking through the room as she stepped closer to Karma.

Karma didn't flinch; her posture remained relaxed, and her eyes were half-lidded with disdain.

"Only compared to some."

Selena's jaw clenched, and her fists shook as she balled them up, struggling to keep her anger in check. The tension rolled off her, and her glare locked onto Karma, every muscle tense, like she was about to explode at any second.

"What did you just say to me, bitch?"

Karma's smirk grew. "Go ahead, throw another fit. Maybe they'll make you queen of the nuthouse."

Selena surged forward, fists swinging, but Karma barely moved. She sat there, completely unfazed. Violet jumped up, shoving Selena back before she could land a hit.

"Back off, Selena!" Violet barked, stepping between them, fists ready to fight. "You're always looking for a reason to start something!"

Selena shoved Violet back, her face twisted with anger. "Maybe because none of you have the guts to give me a real fight!"

Karma snorted and stood up lazily. She brushed off her

pants like the whole situation was beneath her.

"You two gonna kiss? Should I grab some popcorn for this little soap opera?"

Selena's attention snapped back to Karma. "What the fuck? You got a death wish, new girl?"

Karma rolled her eyes again, folding her arms across her chest. "Please. If I wanted to die of boredom, I'd listen to you yap all day."

Selena sprang forward, her whole body tense and ready to strike, but Dr. Conner burst into the room before she could get far. Her sharp and commanding voice cut through the chaos, bringing everyone to an abrupt stop.

"You're not as tough as you think, pendejo," Karma muttered, finally locking her eyes on Selena with a look so sharp it could cut glass.

Selena let out a harsh, mocking laugh. "From the looks of it, you're the one who's not as tough as she thinks she is." She took another step forward, her grin widening, clearly enjoying every second.

Before things could spiral again, Violet cut in, shouting,

"Shut up, Selena! You're always running your mouth." Selena whirled around on Violet, her eyes blazing.

"What are you gonna do about it, slut?"

Violet didn't back down—she had worked herself up enough in her head to get in a fight.

"You wanna find out?"

"Dudes," Coco interjected, her soft voice barely audible over the rising tension. "Chill out."

Karma sighed again, crossing her arms. "This whole place is a circus," she muttered, shaking her head.

The next second, Violet ran at Selena, fists swinging wildly. "You dumb cunt!" she yelled, hitting Selena with full force.

Selena blocked the first punch, but Violet's next jab landed hard in her ribs. Selena doubled over for a second before snarling and shoving Violet back with enough strength to send her stumbling.

"Come on, Violet! Is that all you've got?" Selena taunted, cracking her knuckles and moving in for another round.

Violet steadied herself, glaring at Selena, ready for another go.

The room was a powder keg on the verge of exploding when Karma stepped in, her shoulders tight but her expression utterly bored.

"You're both idiots," Karma said, her voice steady, cutting through the madness. "You know that, idiots?"

Selena, breathless and looking a mess, snapped her head around, glaring at Karma. "You're the fucking joke here." Karma locked eyes with her, smirking. "You're like a feral animal."

"What the fuck does that mean?" Selena stuck out her chin.

"Ladies," Dr. Conner called out. "I'll bring in the orderlies if you can't control yourselves."

Selena took a step forward. "You think you're better than us?"

Karma raised an eyebrow. "Oh, please, bitch. You couldn't handle me—you wish. You think I'm scared of you?"

Selena's body trembled with rage, but before she could strike, Dr. Conner stepped forward again, her presence commanding.

"Girls," she called out, her voice louder and firm.

Violet rubbed her chin, glaring from the sidelines, while Selena stood poised, still ready to fight. The other girls shrank back, unsure of what would happen next.

Dr. Conner crossed her legs and sat on the chair in the middle of the circle. She had calmed and looked around as if nothing had happened, de-escalating the situation.

"How are we feeling today?" she asked in a probing, measured tone.

"Fantastic," Karma deadpanned, flopping back into her chair with an exaggerated sigh. "Best day of my life."

Dr. Conner's gaze shifted between the girls, sensing the anger still simmering beneath the surface. "Let's talk about what happened yesterday," she said softly, her eyes on Violet.

"Violet, would you like to start?"

Violet glared at the floor, refusing to speak, her jaw set like stone.

Dr. Conner nodded, her attention moving to Karma. "Karma, I like it when new patients share."

Karma stretched out, folding her arms across her chest.

"Nope. I'm good."

Dr. Conner sighed, clearly aware Karma wasn't going to budge. She turned to Selena, who was still seething.

"Selena, how are you feeling?"

Selena wiped her mouth with the back of her sleeve, her eyes flashing with frustration. "I feel like punching something."

Dr. Conner raised an eyebrow, her gaze steady. "Anything else you'd like to share?"

"Yeah," Selena said, breathing heavily, her eyes flicking between the girls. "This place is full of losers."

Karma chuckled softly, her voice dripping with sarcasm.

"Right, because you're a winner."

Selena's gaze dropped to Karma's split lip and swollen cheek, her face hard. "Funny, coming from someone who looks like Louise already handled you."

Karma's smirk didn't falter. "You're all talk, no action.

So, go ahead—try me."

Selena's grin tightened, her fists clenching as she took another step closer. "You think I won't?"

Karma's expression remained boring. "Well, you're quite the asshole. But I could always humor you if you're desperate to lose a fight."

Before things could escalate further, Dr. Conner stood up, her tone sharp, leaving no room for debate.

"That's enough. We need to find a way to coexist here."

The orderlies shuffled into the room and moved between the girls as the tension slowly began to ease. Dr. Conner took a deep breath, composing herself.

"We need to work through these emotions more healthily," she said.

Coco, who had been silent the whole time, finally spoke, her voice trembling.

"I miss the ocean."

Dr. Conner immediately turned to her, nodding for her to continue. "Tell us more, Coco."

"I miss everything about it," Coco said quietly, her voice shaking. "The smell, the warmth, how it made me feel... peaceful."

Selena rolled her eyes and groaned loudly. "Here we go again."

Coco curled her toes, trying to steady herself. "You don't know a damn thing about me, Selena," she snapped, her voice trembling.

Selena's entire body went rigid, shoulders tight, fists ready to strike. The orderlies shifted, watching closely. But Karma didn't react; she watched Selena tense up like it was entertainment.

Selena leaned forward, a cruel smile playing on her lips.

"Coco, you miss the ocean? Maybe they'll put you in a fish tank, where you belong."

The other girls burst into laughter, their mocking voices filling the room. Coco's face flushed, and she curled her toes, staring at the floor.

Dr. Conner stepped forward once more, raising her hand.

"That's enough. We are all here to heal, starting with respecting each other."

The room hummed, and the chaos slowly ebbed away. Selena sat back, still panting, her eyes locked on Karma with vicious intent. The other girls shifted uneasily, trying to act normal, as an uneasy stillness settled over the room.

Karma, completely unbothered, stretched lazily in her chair, her arms over her head as if nothing had happened.

"So… can I go to the bathroom now?" she asked, sounding completely bored.

Dr. Conner hesitated for a moment, studying Karma's face. She could still feel the heat in the room but remained confident. "Go ahead, Karma," she said calmly. "We'll continue when you return."

Karma swaggered toward the door, each step lazy and unhurried.

Dr. Conner straightened her posture, turned back to the group, and continued with a composed smile. Despite the eruption, she remained confident that they could regain control.

"Now, let's refocus."

Don't Wait Up!
Group
Group Sessions
G-250
Room #5
Session #10
Group #3

CHAPTER 10

FUGITIVE HEARTS

Karma drifted down the empty hallway, her steps uneven and slow, eyes locked on the floor as she scuffed her rubber-soled shoes along the unpolished vinyl. The squeak bounced off the walls, breaking the silence, but she barely noticed. She kept moving, lost in the rhythm of the sound, each step a careless drag against the shiny surface.

"Karma!"

A voice called out, but she kept walking, head down, lost in her world.

"Karma!" The voice came again, sharper this time.

She glanced up to see Eve a few feet ahead, holding the door open and gesturing for her to follow.

"Come here," Eve whispered, her hand flicking urgently.

"Come on, I got a phone!" Her eyes sparkled with excitement, and a grin spread across her face.

Karma's expression shifted instantly, a mischievous glint lighting up her eyes. She quickened her pace, arms swaying easily at her sides, a casual swagger in every step. Her grin spread, tugging at her split lip, but she barely noticed the sting.

Eve held out a small black flip phone, passing it to Karma with a conspiratorial smile. "You needed to use a phone?"

Karma snatched it eagerly. "Where'd you get this?"

Eve smirked. "I told you, for the right favor, you can get anything."

Karma cocked an eyebrow. "Yeah? What kind of favor did you do to get it?"

Before Eve could respond, Karma's fingers were flying across the keypad, dialing swiftly. She squinted at the screen, ensuring she dialed the correct number.

The phone rang... but no one picked up. A voicemail clicked on.

"Hey, this is Cole. You know what to do."

"Fuckin' shit," Karma muttered.

The phone buzzed a second later—an incoming text message.

(Text Message): Who is this?

"Yeah, that's him," Karma muttered.

(Text Message): It's Karma.

She drummed her fingers on the screen, her foot tapping impatiently.

(Text Message): Where are you?

"Karma! Karma!" Nurse Stone's voice echoed down the hall. Eve's eyes darted to the corridor, alert and anxious.

(Text Message): Babe, I'm at my place. Where the hell are you?

The rhythmic click of Nurse Stone's shoes grew louder, her steps quick and closing in fast.

"Karma, you need to stop this!" Nurse Stone's voice grew closer, her tone stern and commanding.

"Shit!" Karma hissed, her fingers moving quickly over the keys as she scrambled to send another message.

(Text Message): I need to meet up with you. What's the address?

KNOCK, KNOCK. Nurse Stone rapped on the door with her knuckles, each knocking firmly and authoritatively.

"Hello? Who's in there?" Nurse Stone called out.

(Text Message): Come to my place. House on the corner, remember? BRING MONEY. LOVE YOU, BABE.

(Text Message): Love you, miss you, Karma quickly typed.

Karma tossed the phone back to Eve, who quickly stuffed it down the front of her pants and tucked it away.

KNOCK, KNOCK, KNOCK. Nurse Stone banged hard on the door.

"Karma! Open this door." Her voice was sharp, with an edge that hinted she wasn't buying any excuses.

Eve unlocked the door and cracked it open, attempting to look nonchalant. But Nurse Stone stood in the doorway, arms crossed, her face rigid with irritation, and her eyes narrowing as she assessed the situation.

"Karma, they're waiting for you in your group session," Nurse Stone barked, blocking her path with a firm arm. "Yeah," Karma muttered, slipping past without a second glance.

"Eve, find something else to do. Karma, get back to your session," Nurse Stone ordered.

The girls split up, walking in opposite directions while Nurse Stone followed Karma at a distance.

Dr. Conner was mid-lecture when Karma sauntered in and flopped into her seat.

"Alright, welcome back, Karma," Dr. Conner said with a hint of forced patience. "I never officially introduced Karma to the group."

Karma, unamused, braced herself for the inevitable group-sharing ritual.

"How do you feel today?" Dr. Conner asked, trying to engage.

Karma's expression remained blank. "Like getting the fuck outta here," she replied without hesitation.

Violet chuckled softly. "You and me both."

Dr. Conner tried to steer the conversation in a different direction. "Let's focus on something else. Karma, why don't you tell us something about yourself?"

"I'm just peachy, thanks," Karma replied with mock sweetness, glancing at Coco with a smirk.

"Maybe start with something you enjoy," Dr. Conner pressed, trying to keep the discussion productive.

Karma rolled her shoulders, her gaze defiant. "Drugs. I like getting fucked up on drugs," she said, licking her lips provocatively.

The room erupted with cheers and laughter. The girls whooped and hollered, their excitement filling the space. Karma leaned back, grinning wickedly, running her tongue across her split lip as she stared down at Dr. Conner, daring her to react.

Dr. Conner's composure slipped for a moment as frustration broke through. She snapped her binder shut with a sharp thwack that echoed through the room.

"Alright, that's enough," she said, her voice tight with irritation as she stood up.

"This is not what this group is about."

Sensing the tension rising, the attendants edged closer; concern etched on their faces.

"Ladies, our session is over for today," Dr. Conner announced, a note of disappointment coloring her words. She paused, letting the silence settle as her eyes crossed the room. Her gaze lingered on each face as if trying to read the emotions simmering beneath the surface, assessing the tension in the air. "We'll continue this discussion at our next meeting," Dr. Conner said, a hint of forced optimism in her tone. Her eyes lingered on Karma, who met her gaze, a smirk playing on her lips, utterly unfazed by the fiction still pulsing through the room. With a final, defiant look, she let the silence speak for her, leaving Dr. Conner's words to fade into the background as the moment stretched and she disappeared out the door.

KARMA AND EVE

18
Get out!

CHAPTER 11

KARMA'S EDGE

Karma lounged on her cot, her legs draped lazily over the edge, dirty bare feet hanging off the side. She watched Eve, who sat on her bed, nose buried in the same dog-eared book she always read.

"Hey!" Karma blurted.

"Yeah?" Eve responded without looking up.

"Why don't you have to go to group sessions? Where'd you get that phone earlier? And what's with you always lugging around that goddamn book?" The questions shot out like lightning, rapid and sharp.

Eve blinked as if snapping out of a trance, her eyes refocusing as she slowly grounded herself in the real world.

"They don't make me go anymore. I've been here too long," Eve said, closing the tattered pages of her book and giving

Karma her full attention.

"Why've you been here so long?" Karma pressed.

Eve hesitated, her gaze distant as old memories pulled at her. "Lots of reasons," she finally said, her voice soft, almost lost.

"Like what?" Karma leaned forward, sensing something deeper.

The room grew quiet, an uncomfortable silence settling between them. Karma stared at Eve, waiting for her to continue.

"Well?" Karma winked.

Eve sighed, the shadow of her past creeping into her voice.

"I was moved around to a lot of different foster homes, and stuff happened."

"Like what stuff?" Karma's eyes were wide, waiting like a gossip-hungry kid.

Eve's expression hardened. "Well, I lived with a pastor's family, and at night, he would... um, touch me."

"Pig," Karma muttered. "I hate religious freaks."

Eve shifted uncomfortably. "When I told his wife, she called me a liar and locked me in the basement for a long time."

"What a cunt," Karma pretended to spit.

Eve's eyes glazed over, her mind trapped in the memories.

She could feel the cold dampness of that basement, the suffocating isolation, and the anger in the pastor's wife's voice. Even now, the wounds felt fresh, never fully healed.

"She accused me of being a slut," Eve continued, her voice hollow. "She said it was my fault, that I was a sinner. She said all kinds of horrible things to me."

Karma watched as Eve zoned out, lost in her thoughts.

"Ahem-hem." Karma cleared her throat, snapping Eve back to the present.

"They found me tied up down there a few weeks later," Eve said, sitting up.

"Turns out, Pastor Graham's wife had killed him. Left him to rot in their bed until the smell finally got someone's attention."

Karma's eyebrows knit together. "Wow, that took a wild turn."

"Yeah," Eve replied, her voice hollow. "And it wasn't the only crazy thing that's happened to me either. I've been stuck here ever since."

"You live here?" Karma asked, her tone shifting, a hint of curiosity sneaking in.

Eve nodded. "Yeah, until I turn eighteen."

"Then what?"

She shrugged, uncertainty clouding her face. "Then I'm on my own. I'll have aged out of the system, so they'll kick me out."

"So when is that?" Karma asked, more engaged. "How old are you?"

"I turn eighteen next week," Eve answered.

"No shit... What are you going to do?"

"Not sure. Wherever life takes me, I guess." She shrugged

again.

They sat silently for a moment, their eyes meeting with a flicker of understanding. Karma felt a shiver crawl down her spine, her body giving a slight tremor before she finally broke the quiet.

"Can I get a couple more pills?" she asked, her tone casual but laced with quiet urgency.

Eve nodded and reached under her mattress. Her fingers brushed against the rough fabric until she found the familiar plastic pill container. She pulled it out and handed it to Karma with a slight smile. "Check this out," she said, pointing to a tiny, scratchy etching on the lid—a rough sketch of a skull with a "poison" logo.

"Cool, huh?"

Karma leaned forward, taking the container. She glanced at the lid, her expression barely changing.

"Yeah, it's pretty cool," Karma muttered, her tone indifferent as she stared at the etched skull. She stood up slowly, her shadow stretching long across the dim room. Moving over to sit beside Eve, she opened the container with a soft click, tipping the pills into her palm. Her eyes studied them, rolling one between her fingers before finally speaking.

"We gotta get out of here," Karma said, the words low but laced with urgency. She didn't look at Eve right away, her focus still on the pills, as if they were somehow part of the escape plan.

Eve shifted uncomfortably. "I don't know about that," she said quietly, a slight tremor in her voice. "I mean, what would we even do? Where would we go?"

Karma looked up, her expression hardening as she met Eve's gaze. "What do you mean, 'where would we go'? You're getting kicked out soon anyway. What's the difference?" Her voice sharpened, frustration creeping in. "You'd rather stay here, waste away like the rest of these losers?"

Eve blinked, caught off guard by the intensity in Karma's voice. "It's not that simple. You think just running will fix everything?" she asked, her tone soft but steady. She glanced down at the pills in Karma's hand. "What happens when we get caught?"

Karma frowned, leaning in closer. "What the fuck do you care? You said it yourself: they're throwing you out when you turn eighteen. You're on your own, just like me. We could help each other, Eve. We don't need this place. We don't need anyone."

Eve's lips parted, but no words came out. She couldn't tear her eyes away from Karma—something in her stare, fierce and unyielding, made it hard to argue.

The way Karma's eyes flashed with determination, it was as if she'd already decided for both of them.

"I don't know, Karma..." Eve's voice wavered, her fingers fidgeting with the edge of her blanket. "Where would we even go?"

Karma leaned back slightly, her gaze softening, but the urgency remained. "Anywhere but here," she said, her tone quiet but filled with conviction. "There's a whole world out there, Eve. We can figure it out."

Eve swallowed hard, torn between the known's safety and the unknown's pull. "And what if it all goes wrong?"

Karma shrugged, a grin tugging at her lips.

"At least we can try. It beats rotting away in this place." "Where?" Eve asked.

Karma placed a firm hand on Eve's shoulder. "Anywhere but here. We'll vanish into the night, leave this bullshit behind.

We'll be like... sisters."

Karma could see the word struck a chord with Eve. She knew she could manipulate her with that idea—Eve was desperate for a friend, for family. It was written all over her face, in the way her eyes lit up at the mention of "sisters."

"Sisters?" Eve's eyes lit up at the thought.

"Soul sisters!" Karma echoed with a grin, leaning into the manipulation.

"Run away?" Eve stammered.

"Disappear," Karma corrected, her voice relaxed and confident.

Eve began pacing the room, her hands gesturing anxiously.

"I don't think it's a good idea, Karma."

Karma glared, growing visibly upset with Eve's hesitation.

"You wanna stay here?"

Eve bit her lip, then finally asked, "But where would we go?"

Karma handed her back the pill container. "My boyfriend's place first, but after that, anywhere."

"What about money?" Eve asked. "I don't have any. Do you?"

"I'll figure it out," Karma muttered, popping the pills into her mouth. She winced at the bitterness, struggling to swallow as they dissolved on her tongue.

"Wait, stop! Don't take those pills!" Eve cried, jumping to her feet.

"What?" Karma asked, confused.

"Just spit them out! Please!" Eve begged, grabbing Karma's wrist.

"Yo, don't grab me," Karma snapped, yanking her arm away and shoving Eve back.

Eve's voice quivered. "Just spit them out, please!"

Karma hesitated. "What the fu—"

"The orderlies..." Eve's voice cracked. "Sometimes they come into our room at night."

Karma's expression darkened. "What do you mean?"

Eve gnawed her lip harder, struggling to find the words.

"They come in when we're medicated... and do things."

Karma's face went pale. "Say what?"

Eve chewed her fingernail, her anxiety rising. "I've heard them talking... I think they might come in here tonight."

Karma straightened up, her eyes scanning the room in disbelief. "The attendants molest us at night?"

Eve's voice was barely a whisper, her grip tightening around her book. "I don't know... something."

Karma's face twisted with anger. "Why didn't you say anything before?"

"I don't know, I forgot to."

"And you're okay with this?"

"No, I'm not!" Eve replied, her voice trembling. She reached under her mattress again, pulling out a sharp, stubby object—a makeshift shank, jagged and crude in the dim light.

"Here," Eve said, holding it out to Karma. "Sleep with this close."

Karma's eyes widened as she grabbed the shank with a firm grip, twirling it in her hand with ease. She examined the crude weapon, a wild grin spreading across her face.

"Are you serious?" Karma asked, her voice thick with anger.

She waved the shank in the air, the glint of metal catching the light, adding a dangerous intensity to the moment.

Karma's eyes blazed with fury as she hurled the brutal threat, her low, menacing tone daring anyone to take her on. "I dare them to come in here... I'll cut their fucking balls off," she snarled, her voice shaking with rage. The air seemed to vibrate with her anger as if the walls were reverberating from the force of her words.

KARMA AND EVE

MY NAME IS:
DENNIS MUNZO
PSYCHIATRIC WARD : ORDERLY
EMPLOYEE # : 291960

Hey?
Whats
going
on?

ZOINK

N5

CHAPTER 12

NO TURNING BACK

The night dragged on as residents slipped into their rooms, the once-lively corridors fading into silence. The hallways, cloaked in darkness, felt unnerving, broken only by the faint echo of footsteps. A sense of unease lingered as if something was on the verge of happening, yet no one could say what.

Jen sat hunched over at the nursing station on level six, fingers wrapped tightly around the coiled phone cord, twisting it until it dug into her skin. The lights above flickered erratically, casting distorted shapes that slithered along the walls, creeping into every corner. It felt like the darkness was alive, closing in from all sides.

The secure double doors opened, and Dennis strolled in. His casual stride echoed ominously down the hall as he approached Jen. His presence cast an oppressive weight over her, and she recoiled in disgust, her face scrunching up.

Startling her, he slammed his hand flat on the desk with a sharp crack.

"Hey, Jenny," he said with a twisted grin.

"Hey, Dennis," she snarked back.

"If you ever want to sneak into one of the empty rooms, I'm your man," he leered, leaning in too close, his stale breath invading her space. Jen pushed herself away abruptly, her chair wheels squeaking across the floor, breaking the moment like a blade slicing through the taut rope.

"Yeah, no thanks," she replied, a forced laugh barely masking her disgust. She wrinkled her nose, trying to shake off the feeling of his gaze lingering on her.

"Your loss," he sneered, his eyes trailing over her as he stepped back. "I'm as good as it gets." His words dripped with a dark insinuation, leaving a dirty chill in the air as he finally pulled away, a smug grin still plastered on his face.

"Yeah, I'm sure. I guess I'll have to take your word for it," Jen replied, rolling her eyes as she put the warm phone receiver to her ear, deliberately ignoring him.

"I'm going to do a lap," Dennis announced arrogantly, tapping the counter before turning away. His footsteps echoed, then faded as he walked toward the end of the hall. Glancing over his shoulder to ensure Jen wasn't watching, he pulled out a key and slid it into the lock of Eve and Karma's room. The door creaked as it opened, and light from the hallway momentarily illuminated the room before he stepped inside and shut it behind him.

Eve lay on her bed, eyes squinting, pretending to sleep as Dennis approached. He reached out to shake her shoulder, but she turned, her gaze meeting his with conflicting emotions.

"Did she take them all?" he whispered, leaning in close.

His eyes narrowed with a twisted curiosity.

"Yeah," Eve nodded, barely audible, her gaze fixed on the floor.

Karma strained to catch what they were saying, but their words were muffled, drowned out by the relentless pounding of her heartbeat. It thudded in her chest so loud it pulsed in her ears, filling her head with a dizzying rhythm. She couldn't shake the feeling that whatever they were discussing wasn't meant for her to hear, which made her want to listen to it all the more.

Dennis moved toward Karma, who lay motionless on her cot, her eyes shut. Her hand, hidden under her stomach, gripped the shank tightly. He reached down and placed his hand on her breast, his fingers digging in.

Karma's mind raced, visualizing her next move. Suddenly, her eyes snapped open—dark and intense like a shark's. With a surge of adrenaline, she sprang to her knees and swung her arm back, launching her fist forward with the shank aimed directly at him.

"What the fuck?!" Dennis yelled, throwing his arms up to block her. Karma's strike missed, but she didn't stop. She pulled her arm back again, this time driving the shank into his neck.

A guttural sound escaped Dennis as the blade pierced his flesh, blood pouring down his collar in thick streams. Karma yanked the shank back, but Dennis rushed forward, knocking it from her hand. The weapon clattered to the floor, skidding out of reach.

Grabbing his bleeding neck with one hand, Dennis lunged at Karma, forcing her to the ground. He wrapped his fingers around her throat, squeezing tightly as her face turned from red to a deep shade of purple. Blood continued to gush from his neck, soaking his uniform and smearing his name tag with red.

From behind, Eve stepped up and drove a makeshift shank into his back, the jagged piece of metal slipping between his ribs. Dennis let out a deep, ragged groan, his body buckling as he fell to his knees. Blood seeped through his shirt, darkening the fabric as he clutched at the wound. His breaths came in ragged gasps, eyes wide with shock and pain, the reality of it hitting him hard.

"Fuck you, bitch..." he muttered, struggling to reach for the shank lodged in his spine.

At the nursing station, Jen remained engrossed in her phone call, oblivious to the chaos unfolding down the hall. The faint sounds from the end of the corridor went unnoticed as she laughed and chatted, safe in her world, leaving the orderlies to deal with the residents.

Back in the room, Dennis curled up on the floor, blood pooling around his head and soaking into his clothes. Karma wrenched the shank out, her grip tight, and drove it back into him again and again, each thrust fueled by raw anger. "You piece of shit," she spat, her voice shaking with fury. "You think you can just—"

Dennis groaned, slurring his words, "Ah...fuck...you psycho," his voice barely audible through the pain. His body contorted in the fetal position; he tried to shield himself, arms weakly pulling in, but she didn't stop. She kept coming, relentless, her blows landing with vicious precision.

She kicked him hard in the face, the impact cracking against bone. "You're nothing," she hissed, standing over him as his eyes rolled back and he finally blacked out, limp and useless on the cold floor.

"What are you doing?" Eve cried, stumbling backward, her eyes wide with shock as she watched Karma's savage violence unfold.

"Fuck this guy," Karma spat, now rummaging through Dennis's pockets. She pulled out his phone and grabbed his keys.

"Is this the phone you had earlier?" Karma asked Eve, giving the small flip phone a stern, suspicious look as she turned it over.

"No," Eve shot back, her tone defensive, arms crossing over her chest.

Karma's eyes narrowed. "Get your stuff. Get dressed. We're getting out of here." She scrolled through the text messages, her expression darkening when she stopped on the last one.

"Then why's my message still on it?" Karma held up the phone, the screen glowing with her final words staring back at them.

Eve's eyes darted nervously. "I got it from someone else," she muttered, shifting uneasily. "I didn't know it was his."

For a second, Eve froze, then sprang into action, scrambling to grab her clothes from the closet. Her hands shook as she pulled on her shoes and yanked a sweater over her head. Karma, already dressed in a T-shirt and jeans, held the phone in one hand and tossed the keyring to Eve with the other.

"Unlock the door," she ordered.

Eve slid the key into the lock, but Karma shoved her aside before she could turn it. "Come on, let's go," she snapped.

Karma crept into the hallway, her eyes scanning the dim corridor, the faint glow from the nursing station barely reaching them. Eve followed close behind, crouching low as they moved toward the staircase.

Karma's hands trembled as she fumbled with the keys, struggling to steady herself. After a moment, she found the right one, slipped it into the lock, and the stairwell door clicked open with a quick twist.

"Nice," she whispered, relief slipping into her voice as they slid inside, closing the door quietly behind them. They bolted down the dark staircase, shadows chasing their every step. Reaching the bottom, Karma threw open the door, and a rush of cool night air filled their lungs. Grabbing Eve's hand, she led her toward the institution's wooded area, toward the staff parking lot.

"Over here," Eve whispered, tugging Karma toward a new direction. "The lot's just past these trees. The car should be nearby."

Karma nodded, following Eve as they reached the lot. She stumbled, hitting the pavement, the keys and phone flying from her hands.

"Shit..." she muttered.

"You okay?" Eve asked, grabbing her arm to help her up.

Karma brushed dirt from her scraped knee. "I'm fine."

"There!" Eve pointed to a white TransAm parked at the far end of the lot.

They hurried toward it, Karma scrambling for the keys and unlocking the door. Eve jumped into the back seat, but Karma yanked her forward. "What the fuck are you doing?"

"What?" Eve needed clarification.

"Get in the front."

"I can't drive," Eve stammered, wide-eyed.

"Passenger side, dumbass!" Karma snapped.

Eve scrambled into the front, and Karma jammed the key

into the ignition. The engine roared to life, the V8 rumbling through the car.

Karma gripped the gear shift, slamming her foot on the gas, but she misjudged the distance and swung the car backward, crashing into a nearby Volkswagen. The impact jolted both girls, their eyes wide in shock and their adrenaline surging.

"Fuck!" Karma hissed, breathing hard as she forced the gears back into place. Eve clutched the seat beside her, her nervous grin faltering.

Karma stomped on the gas, the tires screeching as the car fishtailed out of the lot. Smoke curled from the asphalt, mingling with the cool night air, a ghostly trail of their escape. In seconds, they vanished into the darkness, the facility shrinking behind them, swallowed by shadows as they tore down the empty road, leaving silence in their wake.

KARMA AND EVE

BANG !!!!
BANG ...!

CHAPTER 13

BLOOD IN THE FAMILY

Karma and Eve sat in the Trans Am, the dull hue of streetlights casting long beams over the row houses and brownstones across the street. The city felt as though it were holding its breath, the air thick with tension, the echo of their actions hanging in the silence.

Eve's body was tense, her eyes fixed on Karma as if trying to will herself out of the situation. Her mind spun like a cyclone, thoughts colliding as she struggled to grasp the enormity of what they'd done. The neon signs outside the car flickered like taunting fingers, echoing the chant in her mind: *What have we done? What have we done?* The silence in the car was a living, breathing entity, its weight pressing on her chest.

"I can't handle this," Eve whispered, her voice quivering. Karma took a deep breath, a soft wheeze escaping her lips like a low whistle.

"Do you think we killed him?" Karma asked.

"I-I don't know," Eve stammered, her voice barely a

whisper, each word shaky and uncertain. Her hands fidgeted nervously, and she glanced around as if searching for an escape.

Karma stared out the window, scanning the house across the street. "Yeah, well, who cares? He was a scumbag. He deserved what he got."

The stillness hung heavy between them as they sat in the car, the world outside eerily quiet.

Eve turned to Karma, her face pale. "What are we doing here?"

Karma's mind was miles away, her focus scattered and distant.

"I don't like hurting people," Eve said quietly. "I'm not like that."

Karma's gaze snapped to her, locking onto Eve's with an intensity that made her cringe. Karma leaned forward, gripping Eve's wrist firmly, pulling her closer until their faces were inches apart.

"Aren't you sick of letting people treat you like garbage?" Karma hissed, her words heavy with anger.

Eve stared back, caught in Karma's bloodshot gaze, fear flickering in her eyes. She hesitated, her voice barely steady.

"Yeah, but..."

"But what?" Karma interrupted.

"I don't know," Eve mumbled, her fingers tapping anxiously against her thigh. "I shouldn't have come with you.

I made a mistake."

Karma's face twisted as she swung her arm, her palm smacking sharply against Eve's cheek, leaving a stinging burn. "Oww! What the hell?" Eve yelped, but her protest was cut short as Karma's hand clamped down over her mouth.

"Shut up. Just shut up, bitch," Karma growled, frustration seeping from every pore, her eyes blazing with fury. Eve froze, her breath fast and shallow as sweat beaded her forehead.

"You're not going back," Karma said, letting go and falling back into her seat with a sly smile. She turned to gaze out the window, her eyes fixed on the house across the street. Eve sank deeper into her bucket seat, her hands gripping the edge tightly.

Outside, the low hum of a distant car broke the quiet, its headlights sweeping across the road and casting a silvery glow on the asphalt. A black cat slipped between parked cars, its eyes gleaming like tiny lanterns in the darkness.

Karma tapped her fingers against Eve's chest, breaking the silence with a steady rhythm. "Come on," she said, pushing the door open. The long creak echoed down the empty street.

Eve hesitated, chewing on her lip before finally opening her door and stepping out. Shoulders slumped, she followed Karma across the street and down the narrow path beside a brownstone. Overgrown bushes scratched at them as they moved through the shadows toward the back.

"This way," Karma said, jerking her head toward the rear

of the house. She pushed open a creaky wooden gate and disappeared into the darkness. Bending down, she lifted a flower pot beside the door, her face twisting in frustration as she searched beneath it.

"God damn it," Karma muttered, making Eve tense up.

"What?" Eve asked, shivering.

"They took the spare key," Karma said, her voice irritated. Eve stood frozen, staring blankly at her.

"Go back to the side," Karma whispered harshly, shoving Eve toward the gate. Muttering to herself, "Shit, shit, shit,"Karma slipped past her and headed for a corner window. With a sharp tug, she slid it open, then shot a glare back at Eve. "Oh yeah," she murmured, hoisting herself up.

"That's perfect," she reiterated, pulling herself through the window with practiced ease. She turned back, reached out, and helped Eve climb inside.

They dropped quietly into the dining room, their feet hitting the floor with barely a sound. The room was cloaked in darkness, and they stood still, breaths shallow, listening to the silence that seemed to press in around them.

"What are we looking for?" Eve whispered.

"Shut up and follow me," Karma snapped in a low tone.

They crept through the house, Eve's eyes drifting to the family photographs on the walls. She lingered on one of Karma as a child, her expression softened by the sight of her family.

Karma crept down the dim hallway, signaling for Eve to hold back. Suddenly, the soft chime of a clock echoed, breaking the silence and making them both jump.

Karma tightened her grip on Eve's wrist, leading her slowly up the creaking wooden staircase. Each step seemed louder than the last, the old boards groaning. The railing was rough under their hands, splintered and cracked, and with each shift, it released a faint, unsettling moan that echoed back downstairs. They halted at the top of the landing, holding their breath as the darkness thickened around them. The faint glow from below shifted shadows, giving the hallway an eerie, distorted feel.

"Wait here," Karma whispered, then slipped down the hallway, edging toward the room and peering inside as her eyes adjusted to the dim light. Her father lay sprawled across the bed next to her mother, each deep breath punctuating the stillness with his heavy snores.

She moved silently to the nightstand, her fingers dipping into the worn leather wallet beside him.

Eve watched from the doorway, barely breathing, her heart pounding. Karma eased a few bills from the wallet and set it back down. Her gaze lingered on her dad's sleeping face, scanning for the tiniest twitch, ready to flee at any sign of movement. His breathing remained deep, steady, and undisturbed.

Tiptoeing back to the doorway, she gently pulled Eve into

the hallway, and they moved down the corridor to another room. They stepped into the room on the far right, and Karma glided quietly ahead. Her younger sister, Antoinette, lay asleep in bed, her small face calm and unaware. Karma rummaged through a cubbyhole in the closet, slipping some cash from Antoinette's birthday stash.

"Karma?" a soft voice whispered behind them.

They both turned to see Antoinette sitting in bed, her eyes wide with confusion as she entered the scene.

"What are you doing?" Antoinette asked.

Karma smiled, stuffing the money into her jeans pocket.

"Just borrowing something, sweetie."

Antoinette frowned, pointing at the bulge in Karma's pocket. "Does Daddy know you're here?"

"No, and you're not going to say anything," Karma said, her smile turning cold. "Okay?"

"You shouldn't be here," Antoinette said quietly. "I thought you'd be happy to see me," Karma replied, waving Eve over. "This is my friend Eve."

Eve waved awkwardly. "Hi."

Antoinette glared, her face twisted like a confused puppy. A soft rustling sound from down the hall made Karma tense, her eyes darting toward the door.

"Shhh," Karma hissed, sticking her head out into the hallway, listening intently.

Antoinette crossed her arms, her expression hardening.

"You're supposed to be in the hospital," she said, her tiny voice serious.

"Shut up," Karma snapped, her voice low and tense. "Just shut your damn mouth."

A faint rustling sound came from down the hall, making her freeze. Her eyes fixed on the doorway, she took a step closer, straining to hear.

"That's my money," Antoinette protested.

"Shut up, brat," Karma growled, shaking her in frustration.

The sound of footsteps creaked in the hallway. A shadow moved across the doorway.

"Karma!" Vic's voice boomed as he stepped inside. His pajama bottoms hung low, and a wrinkled white undershirt clung to him, still creased from sleep. His short, dark hair was ruffled, and he held a small pistol. The hammer pulled back, and his finger was dangerously close to the trigger.

"What are you doing here?" His voice was low and threatening, his eyes darting between Karma and Antoinette.

"Pa," Karma muttered, eyeing the gun.

"Who's this?" Vic demanded, leveling the gun at Eve, whose eyes went wide with fear. She stumbled back, pressing herself against Karma.

"Dad, put the gun down," Karma said, her voice shaking though she tried to keep steady. She fumbled awkwardly, her body jittery, her pulse racing.

Vic's gaze hardened. "What the fuck are you doing in your

sister's room?"

"Just visiting." Karma grinned, though it was forced. "This is my roommate, Eve."

"What are you doing here?" Vic demanded again, louder and more forceful.

Karma, jittery and clumsy, made a frantic lunge for the gun. She wasn't fast or smooth—her hand slapped against Vic's arm in a hasty attempt to disarm him. Older and slower, Vic tried to pull back, but his reflexes weren't quick enough.

The gun jerked in his grip.

BANG.

The shot echoed violently in the small room, ricocheting off the walls like a crack of thunder. Vic staggered, his face twisting in horror as he saw Antoinette slump back, a dark stain spreading across her nightgown. His eyes widened, and he let out a raw, guttural cry.

"Antoinette! No!" Vic screamed his voice breaking and rushing toward her.

Karma stumbled back, nearly tripping over her feet, her mind struggling to process what had just happened. Her little sister, the blood, Vic's screams—it all collided inside her head, sending her spiraling. A nauseating wave of guilt slammed into her, rooting her in place. Her pulse pounded in her ears, her hands shaking as she watched Antoinette's wide, confused eyes. *She's hurt... because of me...*

But the adrenaline kicked in, her addict mind buzzing,

scattering her thoughts in a thousand directions. She needed to move. To get out. To survive.

Vic's voice tore through her haze. "What have you done?" He was on his knees beside Antoinette, hands shaking, pressing down on the wound, his panic filling the room like poison. "No, no, stay with me! Stay with me, baby!"

Karma's breath hitched, her throat tight as she looked between her father and sister. Every instinct screamed at her to run, but her feet wouldn't move. The weight of it all pressed down hard on her chest. She couldn't think straight.

"Let's get out of here!" she finally shouted, snapping out of her trance. She grabbed the gun from the floor, fumbling clumsily with it as she checked herself and Eve for injuries.

Her body felt numb, but her mind was racing, jagged thoughts colliding as she spun around toward the door.

They crashed into Ophelia in the hallway, a heavy thud knocking them off balance. Ophelia hit the ground with a yelp, but Karma barely paused, yanking Eve's arm and dragging her down the stairs. Their footsteps thudded heavily, each step echoing through the empty house as they barreled toward the door, the weight of what just happened to chase them into the night.

The door flew open, and they burst out. Karma gripped the gun tightly as they sprinted across the yard, her heart pounding in her chest and adrenaline surging through her veins. Eve's footsteps echoed behind her, and the two dove into the car, slamming the doors shut. Karma jammed the key into the ignition, and the engine roared to life. With a sharp twist, the car lurched forward, tires screeching as they sped down the street, disappearing into the dark city.

Back inside the house, Vic knelt beside Antoinette's bed, blood soaking through his pajamas and undershirt. He cradled her limp body in his arms as Ophelia screamed from the doorway.

"My baby! Antoinette!" Her voice was a desperate wail as she staggered to the bedside.

"Call 911!" Vic shouted, his voice strained, as he held his daughter, blood pooling around them.

"What do I say?"

"Our daughter was shot. Tell them it was two burglars, nothing more."

"Okay, okay," Ophelia stammered, her words shaky as she teetered on the edge of hyperventilating. She stumbled into the hallway, her hands trembling as she dialed the number.

Meanwhile, the Trans Am tore down the grimy downtown streets. Karma gripped the steering wheel, one hand still holding the gun as she extended it toward Eve.

"Take this," she ordered.

Eve hesitated before grabbing the gun, her hands shaking as she nervously aimed it at Karma, uncertainty flickering in her eyes.

"Don't point that at me!" Karma yelled, swatting the gun

away. A loud BANG erupted, and the weapon discharged, tearing a gaping hole in the dashboard, shards of plastic flying everywhere.

"What the fuck!" Karma screamed, jerking the wheel hard.

The car swerved violently, its tires screeching as they narrowly missed a parked car. Karma wrestled with the wheel, forcing it back under control. With a sharp twist, she steadied the Trans Am, the car fishtailing before falling back in line on the road.

Eve dropped the gun onto the floorboard, her whole body trembling. "I didn't mean to! It just went off!" she cried, her voice shaking.

"Jesus Christ," Karma muttered, frustration spilling over.

"We need to find a convenience store."

The car roared through the city streets, low, worn-out buildings lining either side, their windows dark and broken. Flickering streetlights threw erratic light into the vehicle, distorting everything inside.

A few miles later, Karma pulled the Trans Am into an empty gravel lot in front of a Quick-Stop. She cut the engine and leaned back.

"I need cigarettes."

BAD MF

CHAPTER 14

QUICK-STOP

The neon lights from the convenience store cast a hazy red and blue glow, stretching long, distorted shapes across the gravel parking lot, lending the empty lot a quiet, deserted feel.

Inside the Trans Am, Karma and Eve sat motionless as the night closed in around them. A sudden gust of wind rocked the car, making it creak and groan. Eve flinched, her heart hammering in her chest as she glanced over at Karma, her voice barely above a whisper.

"Do we have to do this?"

Karma's frown softened, the hard lines on her face easing. She placed a steady hand on Eve's trembling shoulder.

"We have to, Eve. We need the money," she said, calm and unexpectedly gentle.

Eve looked at her, understanding but still feeling the weight of their decision gnaw at her as Karma extended her hand.

"Pass me the gun."

Eve hesitated, then handed it over. They shared a glance before turning their attention to the store's entrance. "Look," Karma muttered, nodding toward the door.

A Black man dressed like a cowboy emerged from the convenience store. As he strode across the lot to his old Ford truck, the light from a nearby pole caught the rhinestones lining his pants, glinting from various parts of his outfit. "Well, that's something," Karma remarked, raising an eyebrow.

The truck's engine rumbled, and with a burst of speed, it peeled out of the gravel lot.

Karma smiled slyly. "Now's our chance," she said decisively. They opened their car doors in unison, the hinges giving a worn, metallic groan.

Karma stepped onto the gravel and walked around to Eve's side. Eve stood frozen, her feet seemingly glued to the ground.

With a firm nudge from behind, Karma pushed her forward.

"You go first," Karma whispered.

They crossed the lot, climbing the two small wooden steps.

Eve swallowed hard, then pulled open the glass door, the little chime ringing out as she stepped inside. Karma quickly glanced back at the empty lot before slipping in behind her.

The blinding fluorescent lights overhead made them squint as they walked toward the counter. Eve's heart raced. The clerk was a skinny, greasy-haired kid, probably in his late teens, lounging behind the counter with a lazy grin. His beady eyes trailed over the girls as they walked in, lingering a bit too long on their backsides. Eve pretended not to notice, throwing him a quick, forced smile before wandering toward the coolers. She opened the fridge door, grabbed a cold can of cola, and glanced nervously toward Karma, who had picked up a six-pack of beer from a pyramid display. Karma handed the six-pack to Eve, who set it on the counter alongside her drink. Karma lingered a few feet back, partially hidden near the candy shelf. The clerk smirked, his bloodshot eyes narrowing as he leaned toward Eve.

"Got ID for that beer?" he asked, his grin widening. Eve hesitated, her eyes darting to Karma, who gave her an almost imperceptible nod. The clerk leaned in closer, dropping his voice.

"Tell you what," he murmured, his gaze moving down her figure, "if you come back here and do me a little favor, I'll do you the favor of selling you that beer."

Eve's stomach turned, and her forced smile faded. Before she could respond, Karma leaped forward, pulling out the gun and shoving it into the clerk's face.

"Give us all the fucking money," she demanded, her voice cold and dangerous.

The clerk's smirk vanished, and he raised his hands defensively, his face pale. "Ah, fuck…" he muttered, his voice trembling.

"Shut up and give her the cash," Karma ordered, nudging

Eve closer to the counter. Eve reached for the money as the clerk stumbled back, his wide eyes darting between her and Karma. "Stop looking at us, asshole," Karma growled, jamming the gun even closer to his face. He went cross-eyed, staring down the barrel, terrified.

"Take it… take it!" the clerk stammered, panicking as sweat beaded on his forehead and trickled down his face.

"Throw me some smokes, dick licker," Karma barked.

With trembling hands, the clerk unlocked the cigarette case, grabbed a few packs, and handed them over. Karma snatched them up, barely keeping the gun steady in her other hand.

"Don't move," she warned the clerk, who froze.

"Not you," Karma hissed at Eve, swatting her arm. "Keep going."

The clerk remained still, his face drained of all color.

"Your wallet," Karma demanded, her voice sharp.

"I don't have one," he whimpered, blinking nervously.

"Bullshit!" Karma shouted, leaning over the counter with the gun aimed right at his head.

"What's your fucking name?"

"Clyde," he stuttered.

"Unless you want to end up dead, Clyde," Karma sneered, her eyes locked down the barrel. "You'd better hand over your wallet."

Clyde slowly reached into his pocket and pulled out a worn

brown leather wallet, his hands shaking as he handed it over. "Can you just take the cash? I want the wallet back," he pleaded, his voice shaky.

Eve, still dazed, opened the wallet and let out a surprised laugh. Stitched in bold black letters across the front were the words "BAD MOTHER FUCKER."

"That's funny," she said, smirking.

"Pulp Fiction," Clyde muttered.

"What?"

"It's from the movie *Pulp Fiction*."

Karma's eyes narrowed, her grip tightening as she aimed the gun at him.

"I don't watch movies, dork," she snapped, her voice cutting through the air.

"I like it. I'm keeping it." She teased.

"Grab a bottle," Karma commanded, pointing to the stack of whiskey bottles. Eve snatched one by the neck. They both began inching backward toward the door.

"Go," Karma urged, giving Eve a smack on the butt and sending her hurrying outside. The door chimed as it swung shut behind her.

Karma lingered, her eyes fixed on Clyde as she raised the gun, her voice slicing through the tension with icy authority.

"On the ground, hands behind your head. And don't even think about calling the cops."

Clyde, visibly shaking, dropped to his knees, his whole

body trembling as he placed his hands behind his head. Karma stepped closer, her gaze darkening with intent.

"You're lucky today," she hissed. "Stay down and count your blessings."

With a final, piercing look, Karma turned on her heel and strode toward the door. Her footsteps echoed in the tense silence, and she stopped just as she reached the exit. She spun around, raising the gun in a swift, deliberate motion.

BANG!

The shot blasted into the ceiling, raining bits of plaster down and filling the air with the sharp scent of gunpowder. The sound reverberated through the room, and Clyde flinched, pressing himself lower to the ground. Karma's grim smile only widened as she took aim at the six-pack of beer on the counter.

BANG! BANG! BANG!

She fired, blasting each can in succession. Beer sprayed across the counter and the floor, covering everything in a sticky mess. Clyde, terrified and humiliated, crouched on the ground as his pants darkened with a spreading wet stain. His face went pale as he whispered, "Please… just leave."

Karma's eyes gleamed with satisfaction as she lowered the gun. "Didn't catch that, Clyde," she sneered, giving him a hard, final look before returning to the door.

Karma pushed through the exit.

"Woohoo!" she yelled, a wild grin spreading across her face

as she vanished into the night.

Eve sat in the passenger seat, the bottle of whiskey resting between her legs, cash scattered across her lap. Karma raced up to the Trans Am, yanked open the door, and jumped inside. She slammed it shut, breathing hard as she tossed the packs of cigarettes onto Eve's lap.

"Hold these," Karma barked, unscrewing the whiskey bottle and taking a long swig, letting some of the liquor dribble down her chin before wiping her mouth with her sleeve.

"Take it," Karma said, handing the bottle to Eve. Eve took a small, timid sip, then screwed the cap back on and placed it between her legs.

Karma cranked the key in the ignition and slammed the car into gear. The engine growled as they sped out of the lot, tires skidding across the gravel and kicking up dust behind them.

"Whooaa, that was fucking rad!" Karma shouted, slapping the dashboard with excitement. She glanced over at Eve, who smirked shyly.

Karma ruffled Eve's hair playfully. "How did that make you feel?"

"I don't know… fine, I guess," Eve replied, unsure.

"Fine? That was fucking great," Karma huffed. "Give me a smoke."

Eve fumbled with the pack, pulling out a cigarette and handing it to Karma.

"Hey, put it in my mouth," Karma said, leaning her head

toward Eve while keeping her eyes on the road.

Eve placed the cigarette between Karma's lips and struck a match, lighting the tip. Karma took a deep drag, coughing hard as the menthol hit her throat.

"Damn it," Karma gasped, pulling the cigarette from her mouth. "Menthol… gross. Fuckin' asshole."

She spat out the window as the car cruised, the engine rumbling beneath them.

"Karma," Eve said softly over the roar of the engine.

But Karma wasn't listening; she was focused on the road, driving with one hand on the wheel, lost in thought.

"Karma," she tried again, her voice nervous.

"Yeah, what?" Karma snapped, snapping out of it and looking over at her.

"I need a tampon… I just got my period," Eve mumbled, her face red.

"For Christ's sake," Karma groaned, spotting a gas station ahead. She pulled the car into the lot and parked. Without missing a beat, she gripped the gun tightly in her fist, her knuckles whitening as she took a steadying breath.

"Okay, leave it running."

The door slammed behind her as she disappeared into the store. Eve sat, tapping her foot anxiously, waiting.

BANG! BANG!

The explosive sound of gunfire shattered the silence.

Moments later, Karma bolted out of the store, jumped into

the car, and tossed a pack of tampons onto Eve's lap.

"Go time," she shouted, flooring it as a bald man in grease-stained overalls burst out of the gas station with a pistol.

"You won't get away with this!" he yelled, his voice lost to the engine's roar as the Trans Am vanished into the night, leaving a haze of dust and exhaust hanging in the air.

The headlights pushed through the darkness, casting faint glimpses of the empty road ahead while Karma's laughter filled the car, wild and breathless. The man's furious silhouette grew smaller in the rearview mirror, swallowed by the dark.

CHAPTER 15

RESTROOM STRANGER

The car roared through the dark, rewinding roads, its tires gripping the curves with a slight screech before finally breaking onto the open highway. The asphalt stretched out endlessly, swallowed by the night, with only the yellowish headlights piercing through the darkness. The engine sputtered, rattling as it fought to keep up, half a gas tank barely fueling their escape. Thick, black smoke billowed from the muffler, leaving a fading trail as they sped into the unknown, the empty road stretching out like a shadowed tunnel with no end in sight. Karma pressed hard on the pedal, the engine humming steadily beneath them. Beside her, Eve squirmed uncomfortably, shifting as she tried to manage the trickle of blood with a crumpled napkin.

"I need a bathroom," Eve muttered. "Gotta put in this tampon."

"Alright, alright," Karma replied, catching sight of a sign up ahead: Rest Stop, Next Exit.

She veered into the empty rest area, the dim restroom lights barely reaching through the darkness. The Trans Am screeched to an abrupt halt right by the door, tires squealing against the asphalt. Karma nodded toward the restroom, her eyes meeting Eve's.

"Go on, I'll wait," Karma said, her voice flat.

Eve closed the car door behind her as she hurried inside. Meanwhile, Karma slid into the passenger seat, flipping open the phone. She dialed a number and waited.

The voicemail clicked on. "This is Cole; you know what to do." Beep.

Karma scowled and quickly typed out a message. "Hey, it's Karma. I'm heading your way." She sat back, waiting for a reply, eyes wandering as a shadow passed by the car, moving toward the restrooms.

Eve braced herself in the cramped, graffiti-covered stall, her hands shaking as she tried to insert a tampon. Her legs trembled, her mind racing in a manic frenzy. The sharp clack of boots on the cement floor echoed off the restroom walls, growing closer. She squinted through the narrow crack in the stall door, catching a distorted glimpse of someone approaching.

"Karma?" she whispered, her voice barely audible, hoping for her to answer back. But nothing—just the sound of movement.

Then, she looked down.

A pair of scuffed black boots stopped just outside the stall. Eve froze, her breath catching in her throat as every muscle in her body went still.

Tap. Tap. Tap.

Something small, like a penny, tapped rhythmically against the hollow metal door of her stall. Eve's heart pounded, and she swallowed hard.

"Hello?" she said in a low tone, her voice barely steady.

"Someone's in here."

The tapping stopped, leaving the room in heavy silence. The only sound was the slow, steady water drip from the faucet.

The boots remained motionless outside her stall.

"Hello?" Eve called again, her voice rising. A sense of dread crept in as she strained to listen.

Finally, a voice broke through—casual and cold.

"My bad," came the reply.

The boots took a few steps back, and Eve exhaled sharply, her body tense, on edge.

What the hell? she mouthed to herself, keeping silent.

She flushed the toilet and slowly pushed the stall door open, stepping out cautiously. But as she did, a figure filled the doorway, blocking her path.

"Hey," the man said, a twisted grin stretching across his face.

Eve jumped back, pressing herself against the sink.

"This is the girls' restroom," she stammered, her voice wavering, caught in fear.

The man's grin widened, and his greasy hair was plastered in uneven strands across his forehead. Something vaguely familiar marked his face, though it was overshadowed by the slimy, unsettling vibe he gave off. He lunged forward, one grimy hand clamping over her mouth, the other wrapped tightly around her neck.

"Shhh…" he whispered, leaning in close, his stale breath spilling over her.

He pawed at her, his hands roving over her chest and lower back with an ugly familiarity, pressing his body against hers as he rubbed his crotch against her leg, eyes glinting with a sick satisfaction.

Eve tried to scream, but his hand crushed against her mouth, her cries muffled into desperate, trapped sounds.

"Shhh…" he warned, his knife catching the faint light as he brought it closer. Her eyes went wide as he pressed the blade against her skin.

"Keep quiet, bitch," he growled, yanking at her shirt and ripping it at the shoulder.

"Stop!" Eve gasped. But his grip tightened, the knife grazing her neck. "Stop fucking moving, or I'll slit your throat," he snarled.

Suddenly, a voice shattered the silence.

"Hey, fuckhead."

The man turned, startled.

"BLAM! BLAM!" Two shots rang out, narrowly missing him and Eve.

He threw his hands up instinctively, his eyes wide with shock.

"What the fuck?" he yelled, staggering backward.

"Get over here, Eve!" Karma barked, her long fingers steady on the gun, her aim unwavering.

Eve tore herself free, stumbling toward Karma. "Go to the car!" Karma ordered, keeping the gun trained on the man.

Eve hesitated for a split second before bolting out the door, her heart racing as she hit the cool night air. Her breaths came in rapid bursts as she ran. Karma remained behind, eyes locked on the man as she stepped closer, unflinching.

"Give me what's in your pockets," Karma demanded, her voice sharp as she aimed the gun at his face. He fumbled for his wallet, clutching the knife tightly in his other hand.

"And drop that fucking knife."

The man tossed the wallet toward her.

"Now, why'd you go and do that?" Karma muttered, stepping forward to pick it up, the gun steady in her grip.

"You got a car?" she asked.

"A van," he muttered, but as soon as he said it, he lunged forward in a desperate attempt to overpower her.

Karma fired. "BLAM!"

"Ahhhhh…"

The bullet tore into his gut, and he crumpled forward, clutching his stomach. "Ahhh…" he groaned, doubling over as pain ripped through him.

"BLAM!"

Another shot hit his shoulder, sending him crashing to the floor. Blood pooled beneath him as he gasped for breath, his body twitching in agony.

Karma stared down at him, her eyes cold and empty. She saw herself in the mirror—pale, with hollow eyes- brushing a strand of hair from her face with the gun barrel before bending down to retrieve the man's keys. She dropped the knife a few feet away from his twitching form, hurried out of the restroom, and sprinted to the car.

"Grab our stuff!" she shouted at Eve, her voice urgent.

Leaning against the window, Eve straightened up and flung the door open.

"What? Why?" she stammered, her scrambled mind racing.

"We're switching cars!" Karma barked, pointing to a van tucked away in the corner of the lot.

Eve gathered their things, her movements frantic. She darted over to Karma, who was already sliding into the van's driver's seat.

"Where are we going?" Eve asked, climbing in beside her. Karma revved the engine, the muffler sputtering.

"We're heading to my boyfriend's," she declared, tossing the Trans Am's keys out the window and into the darkness.

The van rumbled to life, surging forward as they sped away.

A few minutes later, a beat-up station wagon rolled into the parking lot. A young hippie couple, likely in their late twenties, climbed out, their two children trailing sleepily behind.

"I need to go to the bathroom!" the little girl cried.

She darted ahead, clutching herself urgently as she rushed into the dimly lit restroom, her mother on her heels.

"Ahhhhhhhhhhhhhhhhhh!" the girl's scream pierced the air.

1
ABC 2
DEF 3
GHI 4
JKL 5
MNO 6
PRS 7
TUV 8
*
BALTIMORE CITY POLICE
EVER ON THE WATCH
DEPARTMENT
CASE FILE
Autopsy Report
Today's Date:
Name of Deceased:
Autopsy Case #:
Examiner:
FULL BODY ADULT DIAGRAM (FRONT/BACK)
-2 Girls
-Eve
-Karma
-White trans AM
-psyc ward
-father vic
-victim -Dennis
-elderly
-Stabbing
-Shank

CHAPTER 16

CHENEY & WEBB

The detectives' department in the Baltimore City Police Station was thick with late-night tension. It was nearly dawn, the hour when exhaustion blurred lines, and focus slipped. Phones rang sporadically, cutting into the hum of tired voices, and the smell of stale coffee mixed with the damp scent of concrete, seeping from the walls and floors. Desks were cluttered with crumpled case files, scrawled notes, and discarded coffee cups that had long gone cold.

A whiteboard leaned in one corner, filled with names, addresses, and lines linking cases across Baltimore like a map of the city's underbelly. Every so often, a detective glanced at it, the weight of too many loose ends hanging in the room.

Cheney, nursing a cup of sludge from the ancient coffee machine, barely glanced up as Webb approached, picking up a small plastic dinosaur from Cheney's desk and giving it a once-over. Webb raised an eyebrow, amused.

"You're stuck in the past, Cheney. It's the year 2000, man.

You don't have to drink that diesel fuel you call coffee."

"I'll risk it," Cheney grumbled, smirking into his mug.

"Real coffee is supposed to taste like motor oil, white boy."

"Right, because motor oil is so appetizing, hey you old black bastard." Webb chuckled, getting a little too comfortable with his new partner and leaning back in his chair, crossing his arms.

"I'm going to let you get away with that one, 'cause you look like you stepped out of a boy band," Cheney shot back, gesturing vaguely at Webb's gelled hair and trendy suit.

"Don't be jealous just because I look good doing my job," Webb shot back, giving his collar an exaggerated smoothing.

"Besides, someone's gotta balance out your whole grizzled detective act. . . bullshhhit!"

Webb reached over to Cheney's desk and picked up a small plastic dinosaur someone had left there, turning it over in his hand with a smirk.

"What's this, your spirit animal?" Webb teased, holding it up as if he'd found gold. "Didn't know you had a softer side, Cheney."

Cheney shot him a look, reaching to grab it. "Give me that, it's my grandsons," he muttered, but Webb held it out of reach with a grin, bouncing it in his palm.

"He gave it to me for protection."

Webb laughed. "Ah, that's cute big guy. You could use

some… protection old man."

The shrill ring of the phone interrupted the moment. Cheney's attention snapped back to the task at hand as he reached for the receiver.

"Cheney," he answered, his voice rough around the edges. "Yeah, alright. Send it over."

He hung up and gave Webb a brief nod. "Fax coming in."

Webb sighed dramatically, shaking his head. "Fax? It's almost 2000. Have you ever heard of email?"

Cheney gave him a sideways glance as he shuffled over to the old, humming fax machine. "Sure, I've heard of it. I just don't trust it," he grumbled, pulling the sheets from the tray as they slid out with a mechanical whir.

"That's because you're practically a dinosaur," Webb teased. "Next thing, you'll tell me you don't trust cell phones either."

Cheney grunted, he handed over the papers. "Don't need 'em.

"Pagers work just fine for me," he said, patting the device clipped to his belt.

Webb shook his head, still grinning as he scanned the fax. His smile faded as he took in the details.

"A guy got shot at a rest stop, and they took off with his van."

"That's a state trooper problem." Web said.

"But the twist is! That car was reported stolen from the

psych ward employee on the other call tonight," Cheney said, dropping the file onto the desk.

Webb rolled his eyes. "So that makes it ours."

"Yeah, it's us."

"Great," Webb sighed, leaning back. "We've got a runaway nutcase, a stolen car, and now a shooting. And that little girl shot in Greektown all tonight?"

Cheney's jaw tightened. "Her sister's one of the escapees from that mental hospital. It's all connected."

Webb let out a low whistle, rubbing a hand over his face.

"So, our runaways just turned into attempted murder suspects?"

Cheney nodded the weight of it sinking in. "We're not just chasing a couple of escapees anymore. This just got a lot more serious."

He took a sip of his coffee, setting the mug down with a heavy thud.

"Alright, Pretty Boy. Grab your coat. It's gonna be a long morning. I'm driving."

"Pretty Boy?" Webb laughed, standing up and grabbing his jacket. "Keep it up, Cheney. I'll have you drinking Frappuccinos before this case is over."

Cheney looked at his watch. Five AM. He chuckled dryly, pulling his worn leather jacket over his shoulders. "We have a few hours before anything is open. Let's grab breakfast at Nic's."

The two detectives stepped out into the early dawn, leaving behind the low hum of the fax machine and the hushed emptiness of the station. Outside, Baltimore was just beginning to wake, the first hints of morning light stretching over the skyline. The streets were quiet, holding onto the last remnants of night as the city stirred to life. Cheney and Webb moved in stride, their footsteps echoing off the sidewalk as they set out, ready to chase down the next piece of the puzzle.

Name:
ANTOINETTE
Diagnosis:
GUN WOUND
Doc: Dr. Marty M
Condition: Serious!!!
POP

CHAPTER 17

ECHO'S IN THE HALL

In the cold, early morning hours, Vic stood just outside the hospital entrance, his dress shirt wrinkled beneath a long overcoat that clung to his thin frame. The dawn air was sharp, his breath visible in misty puffs as the first light stretched shadows across the pavement. A cigarette smoldered between his fingers, the ember glowing faintly. His gaze drifted over the waking city, but his mind was anchored to the chaos inside.

He turned back toward the hospital doors, worry etched deep into his face, his eyes hollow and red from a sleepless night. Nurses and patients moved past him like phantoms, barely registering as he crushed the cigarette under his heel. Adjusting his coat, he stepped through the automatic doors, which parted with a soft hiss, pulling him into the cold, fluorescent light of the hospital.

Inside, the buzzing overhead lights cast a harsh, greenish-white glow, making every face appear weary and drained. The air was thick with the smell of bleach and antiseptic—an intense, sterile scent that did little to calm the storm swirling in Vic's gut. He moved slowly down the worn corridor, his fingers brushing against the rough surfaces of trolleys and carts, feeling the weight of years embedded in the walls.

He entered the deserted cafeteria and grabbed two foam cups from the dispenser. The coffee machine sputtered and groaned, releasing a thin stream of dark liquid. He paid the cashier without a word and walked back into the hallway, the heat of the cups warming his cold hands.

The corridor seemed to stretch forever, its dim walls and worn furnishings mirroring his exhaustion. Each step tightened the tension in his chest, the air thick with a sense of impending trouble.

At the end of the hallway, he paused by a slightly ajar door. Inside, a doctor and nurse hovered over Antoinette, his youngest daughter, who lay pale and still in the hospital bed. The room hummed with the soft beeps of heart monitors, the quiet hiss of oxygen, and the low drone of medical machinery. Two empty chairs stood like silent witnesses beside the bed.

Ophelia, his wife, stood near the window, clutching a tissue. Her eyes were red and swollen from crying. Her shoulders slumped, weighed down by fatigue and fear. Vic stepped into the room, brushing against her shoulder. She flinched, her eyes meeting his for a fleeting moment before she turned away, wrapping her arms around herself as she moved closer to the window.

"Ophelia, you need to hold it together," Vic whispered, his voice tight with tension.

"Αν δεν ή σουν εσύ , αυτό το ο πλο δεν θα η ταν στο σπι τι μας…" she hissed in Greek, her voice trembling with anger.

Vic leaned in closer, his voice low. "Keep your voice down," he urged. "Antoinette needs us right now. Don't let them see us unravel."

He glanced toward the hallway, where two police officers talked with a nurse. The nurse pointed in their direction, and Vic straightened. He lifted the coffee cup to his lips, leaving faint marks on the foam as he sipped.

"Why are you blaming me?" he muttered defensively. "This is about Karmela, not me."

Ophelia turned to him, her arms dropping to her sides. "If it weren't for you, Karmela wouldn't have had that gun," she whispered fiercely.

Vic moved closer, his eyes darting back to the officers.

"We've got to play this smart. Just stick to the story," he whispered, reaching out to calm Ophelia.

"Mr. Papadakis," a voice called from the hallway.

Vic looked up to see the two officers approaching, their faces set with determination.

"Stay calm," he murmured to Ophelia. "Let me handle this."

He squared his shoulders and walked toward the officers, Ophelia a step behind.

"I'm Detective Cheney," the taller officer said, his voice steady but commanding. He gestured to his partner.

"This is Detective Webb."

"Good morning, sir," Webb said, his sharp blue eyes probing.

Vic nodded, trying to appear cooperative. "Vic Bouzouki. This is my wife, Ophelia."

Ophelia managed a strained smile, her eyes still brimming with tears.

"We're here about your daughters, Antoinette and… Karma," Webb began, his tone direct. "There are some things we need to clarify."

Vic kept his face neutral, though his pulse quickened. "I already told the officers about the break-in," he replied smoothly.

Cheney flipped open his notepad, his eyes scanning his notes.

"Mr. Bouzouki, your daughter Karma was reported missing from the psychiatric hospital earlier tonight," he stated.

Vic's expression remained calm, but his heart pounded.

"Missing?" he repeated, feigning confusion. "I don't know anything about that. We've been here with Antoinette all night."

Webb stepped closer; his voice edged with seriousness.

"Sir, Karma stabbed an attendant during her escape. She and another patient stole a car to get out. She's armed and dangerous."

Ophelia's hand flew to her mouth, her voice trembling. "No… that can't be true. She's just a child," she whispered, trying to sound genuinely surprised…

Cheney's eyes stayed on Vic. "We know she escaped, Mrs. Bouzouki. And we have reason to believe she may have been the one who broke into your house tonight. Are you sure that's not what happened?"

Vic swallowed, his mind racing. "I had no idea," he lied, keeping his voice steady. "We saw the open window, then found Antoinette… I thought it was some kids trying to break in, nothing more."

Webb leaned in, his voice skeptical. "Some kids who just happened to know where you kept a loaded gun?"

Vic paused, then shook his head. "It didn't even cross my mind," he replied. "I was in shock… My daughter was lying there, bleeding."

Cheney's tone sharpened. "Mr. Bouzouki, we're not playing games here. We know Karma came straight to your house. Why didn't you report it?"

Vic took a slow breath, choosing his words carefully. "I didn't know it was her," he said, staying calm. "I've been trying to keep it together… trying to figure this out." Webb's eyes narrowed. "Figure out what? You know she came to you for help, and you're covering for her. That's a serious offense."

Ophelia's eyes widened, but she remained silent. Vic forced a chuckle. "You're making assumptions, detective. I've got no reason to cover for anyone. Karma's got problems, sure, but this isn't one of them."

Cheney's face was stern. "If you're lying, Mr. Bouzouki, and we find out you're hiding your daughter or protecting her from facing the consequences, we will come down on you with everything we've got."

Vic felt his temper rising. "I don't know what you're talking about."

Webb's gaze didn't waver. "She's a danger to herself and others. And if you're keeping her from us, you're putting her at even more risk."

Vic's eyes narrowed, his patience thinning. "I'm not saying another word without my lawyer."

Cheney nodded, though his eyes remained cold. "Get your lawyer, Mr. Bouzouki. But know this—we're not going away until we have Karma in custody. If you stand in our way, you'll go with her."

Vic's jaw clenched, tension tightening in his chest like a vice. He needed to act fast, to find Karma before the cops did.

Every second was precious, and he knew time was running out.

TRY
JUST A LITTLE

CHAPTER 18

DUST AND DESPERATION

Karma reached over and twisted the radio knob, letting the music fade into a low hum. The quiet crept in, thick and heavy, as the van rolled down the residential street. She scanned the row houses on either side, their windows dark and curtains drawn, before tucking the van into the deep shadows beneath a sprawling red maple. The faint, cold gray light of dawn seeped through the trees, casting a dull glow over the damp leaves clinging to the windshield. Inside, the air was thick with the smell of gasoline and wet earth. She grabbed the bottle from Eve, twisted off the cap, and took a long swig, feeling the burn of the liquor slide down her throat, warming her from the inside as the first light crept into the new day.

Eve held a cigarette between her dirty fingers, the ember glowing like a tiny beacon in the dark. With a sly grin, Karma nudged her shoulder, knocking Eve lightly against the passenger window with a dull thud.

"Come on, "Karma muttered, her voice edged with impatience.

They fumbled with the van doors, finally pushing them open and stepping out into the cool morning air on this quiet, vacant street. This neighborhood on the southern outskirts of Maryland felt almost forgotten—heading toward Virginia yet still clinging to the city's rough edges.

The block stretched out before them, lined with worn-out row houses. Some were boarded up, their porches sagging and lifeless, while others showed signs of resilience. A few scattered lights glowed dimly behind frayed curtains, hinting at early risers or restless souls still awake from the night's mischief.

Graffiti covered the old brick walls, and bits of litter collected along the cracked sidewalks. A faint, musty scent of mildew lingered in the air, mingling with the dampness of the morning. They shuffled forward, their footsteps scraping against the concrete, echoing through the hollow shells of abandoned homes. Now and then, a dog barked from a backyard, and the faint murmur of a radio drifted from somewhere—a haunting reminder that there was still life on this forgotten block.

Karma reached for the bottle, taking it from Eve, but didn't drink immediately. She held it in her hand, feeling the cool glass against her skin, her grip tightening as though holding onto a decision. After a moment, she sighed, took a swig, and handed it back to Eve.

Eve took the bottle, wrapping her fingers around it and

raising it to her lips for a small sip, wincing at the sharp, bitter taste. Karma watched her, a hint of amusement in her eyes, then held out her hand, fingers wiggling for the cigarette.

"Smoke," Karma said.

Eve took a drag before passing it over, the orange ember glowing faintly in the morning light.

"Are these people OK with us showing up this early?" Eve asked.

"Oh, I'm sure they're still up. And it's not just some people—it's my boyfriend."

Karma took the cigarette, pressed it to her lips, and inhaled deeply, letting the smoke fill her lungs. She exhaled slowly, watching it drift into the morning air as a familiar burn settled in her chest. Her eyes darted around, restless and unfocused, the alcohol blurring her vision. Shapes wobbled, melting into the dim light as she scanned the block. At the far end, a run-down house loomed, its yard littered with car parts, broken furniture, and heaps of trash spilling onto the cracked pavement.

The stairs creaked beneath their weight as they climbed onto the weathered porch, splinters jutting from the wood, catching the dull morning light. The house looked abandoned, but Karma knew better. She knocked once, waited a moment, then hit again, her patience stretching thin. After a pause, footsteps shuffled down the hallway. Her gaze drifted to the grimy, cream-colored curtain in the side window, which shifted as if someone were peering out. Finally, the door creaked open, revealing a shadowy figure on the other side.

Music played inside, a low beat pulsing in the background. A skinny guy with long, messy blond hair hovered in the doorway, his face pallid and tinged with a sickly yellow hue. Draped in a threadbare, faded robe that hung loosely on his bony frame, he wore a sleeveless undershirt, the thin fabric barely hiding his pierced nipples.

He pushed his hair out of his eyes, giving them a quick once-over with a bored, unfazed look.

"Hey, Jackson," Karma said, flashing a devilish grin.

He barely acknowledged her, muttering, "Yeah?"

"It's Karma… Cole's girlfriend," she clarified, her grin fading, her patience souring at his attitude.

Jackson's expression changed from boredom to mild irritation. "Oh, hey. What's going on?" he replied, a hint of annoyance in his voice.

Karma stepped back, holding up the bottle with a mischievous head tilt. "Where's Cole? He knows I'm coming," she said.

He shrugged, barely looking at her. "He's out. Thought you were locked up in some psych ward or something."

"Yeah, something like that," Karma replied, unfazed, facing his eyes steadily.

Jackson smirked, his lips curling with barely concealed amusement, clearly enjoying the tension.

"This is Eve," Karma added, gesturing to her friend. "Isn't she adorable?"

Jackson's eyes shifted to Eve, giving her a slow, appraising once-over. "Cute enough, I guess," he mumbled, his tone laced with interest, making Eve shrink back a little.

"I need to pick up. I've got money," Karma insisted.

"Oh, do you know?" Jackson replied, narrowing his gaze as he looked her over. "Don't you owe me money?"

"You wish, fucker."

He stared, his eyes flicking back and forth between Karma and Eve, sizing them up with a look that lingered.

"Come on," Karma urged, her eyes wide with desperation and determination. She glanced back at Eve, who looked like a deer in the headlights.

"OK, come in," he finally said, stepping back to let them in.

Karma turned and followed, motioning for Eve to come along.

"Come on," she whispered, tugging Eve's arm.

She closed the door behind them, trapping them in the thick, suffocating air that reeked of chemicals, stale smoke, and rotting garbage. The house was a chaotic mess, barely holding itself together. Yellowed walls, stained from years of nicotine, peeled away in patches like old, dead skin.

The hallway light was burnt out, a faint sliver filtering through a small window on the back wall. As they moved deeper inside, the muffled voices and laughter grew louder, echoing like distant cries. The living room was a mess of broken furniture and discarded trash. In the center, a tattered couch slouched, its stuffing spilling out like the guts of a carcass. Dirty laundry sprawled across the floor, tangled with crumpled fast-food wrappers, half-eaten takeout, and ashtrays overflowing with cigarette butts. A worn, stained rug lay askew over the warped floorboards, barely holding the chaos together.

A wiry girl hovered over a coffee table, snorting a line of speed, her fingers twitching nervously. She glanced up, her eyes bugged out, a crazed grin breaking across her face.

"Karma!" she screeched, her voice cutting through the heavy beat of the music.

Sheena sprang up, her movements sharp and erratic, high as a kite. "Babe! How are you?" she squealed.

Two guys, engrossed in their video game, barely noticed the commotion. One knocked over a beer, spilling liquid over a pile of crumpled papers scattered across the table.

Jackson stepped closer, his face inches from Karma's.

"Where's my money?" he sneered.

"Dude, I don't owe you shit," Karma shot back.

Sheena pushed him back with a grin. "Oh, fuck off, Jackson," she said, draping an arm around Karma's shoulder and nudging her playfully. "Come on."

Karma signaled to Eve, who followed close down the hall

and into a cramped little bedroom. They found an unmade bed shoved against the wall and an open suitcase with clothes and makeup strewn across the grimy, brown carpet. A faint, musty odor clung to the fibers.

"This is Eve," Karma said, nudging her toward Sheena, who lounged on the bed with a twitchy, restless energy.

"Hi," Eve mumbled, barely audible.

"I'm Sheena," she replied with a quick wink, though her hands shook as they fumbled with the zipper of her jacket. Her eyes darted from corner to corner, flitting over shadows and doorways as if she expected someone—or something—to appear at any moment. She glanced back at Eve, then flicked her gaze away just as quickly, shifting uneasily on the bed, her leg bouncing nervously.

Suddenly, Sheena sprang up, pacing back and forth with frantic, jerky steps. Her fingers tapped an erratic rhythm against her thigh, and her breath came in short, quick bursts as if she couldn't get enough air.

"You got any dope?" Karma asked, pulling a few crumpled bills from her pocket.

"I only got meth, but Jackson's holding," she shot back, her jaw clenched tight. Her eyes, sharp and restless, darted around the room, flicking to every corner, every shadow like she was seeing things that weren't there. A full day of being awake had her on edge, paranoia creeping in with every twitch and flicker of her gaze.

Sheena took a swig from the bottle and passed it. They all drifted over to the bed. Sheena and Eve perched on the edge of the mattress while Karma knelt on the floor, smoking and reaching for the booze.

"So, what happened to you? I heard you tried to kill yourself?" Sheena asked, her eyes dilating.

"Yeah…" Karma admitted.

Sheena took a drag, her eye flickering between Karma and her cigarette.

Suddenly, they heard the front door open and slam shut seconds later, sending a shockwave through the house.

"Cole!" Karma jumped up, ran out of the room, and sprinted down the hall, spotting a shadow slipping into a room by the kitchen.

"Cole!" she called out again, marching toward the door, Eve trailing behind her.

Inside, Cole stood in the murky glow, his jacket hanging off his strung-out shoulders, his arms wrapped tight around a dirty-blonde punk girl. Their bodies tangled, and their mouths fused in a messy, desperate kiss like they were trying to consume each other.

"Cole!" Karma's voice cut through the room like a whip. She grabbed him by the collar, yanking him back so hard he nearly fell over.

"What the hell?" he stammered, his face going ghostly pale.

"Karma... babe, what are you doing here?" His voice shook

like a kid caught red-handed.

"Don't you 'babe' me!" she snarled, her eyes cutting into him. "Who the hell is this?"

"She's a friend, babe," Cole mumbled, barely meeting her gaze. "Someone I was helping out."

Karma let out a bitter laugh, her lip curling.

"Helping out? Or helping yourself to?" Her hands balled into fists at her sides, seconds away from throwing a punch.

Eve hovered in the doorway, feeling like she'd walked into something she couldn't back out of. Sheena sidled up to Eve, tipping back a half-empty bottle, grinning like she was watching the best show in town.

"She works for Cole, sweetheart," Sheena said with a mocking drawl.

Karma's head whipped around to face Sheena. "Doing what?" Sheena's grin widened, and she made a crude gesture, chuckling. "She's a trick."

"Shut up!" the punk girl spat, her eyes narrowing as she stepped forward, fists clenched.

"Make me, slut," Sheena fired back, her voice cold and daring.

Sheena feigned a lunge at the girl, stopping just short. Cole jumped between them before she could follow through, shoving them apart with a sharp push.

"Twig, get the hell out of here. Go back to your sister's place or something," he growled, gripping her arm and steering her toward the exit.

"You're a dick," Twig shot back, flipping him off as she stumbled toward the door.

Karma pulled out a cigarette with shaky hands, her eyes never leaving Cole.

"What's this, Cole? You a pimp now?"

His head jerked up, his face flushing.

"I'm not a pimp, babe."

He watched as Twig disappeared down the hall, his jaw clenched.

Twig stormed down the hallway, her footsteps heavy, echoing through the house. She reached the front door, threw it open quickly, and stepped out without looking back. The door slammed shut behind her, reverberating like a final, defiant statement through the house.

"I swear, babe, I missed you," Cole pleaded, reaching for her, softening his voice.

Karma hesitated, her face hard as if weighing every option, every lie… but then she let him pull her in. Their mouths crashed together in an angry, hungry kiss, filled with all the things they didn't want to say.

Eve stood a few feet away, her stomach twisting. The noise from the other room was rising—shouting, laughter, the messy thrum of chaos and broken lives. Sheena leaned against the doorway frame, a smug grin on her face.

Cole's hands moved over Karma's back, clinging to her like

a life raft. His voice was a low murmur against her skin.

"Let's get high," he whispered, guiding her toward the bed, his fingers already twitching with anticipation.

He crouched, pulling a small, beat-up metal box from under the mattress. The lid creaked open, revealing twisted plastic bags of brownish-white powder, burnt spoons, and bent needles.

"I need a rig," he muttered, snapping his fingers like he was calling a dog.

Eve's heart pounded in her chest, her mouth dry.

"I don't want to do that," she whispered, her voice swallowed by the thick air.

Karma's eyes flicked over to her, softening briefly before darkening again.

"You'll be fine," she muttered, though something cold crept into her tone, something that didn't feel right.

Sheena laughed, a harsh sound that turned into a cough, bouncing off the walls. "Yeah, Eve, come on… just one taste.

Don't be such a baby," she taunted, her grin dark and dangerous. Eve felt the room closing in, the walls pressing tight and wondered if this was the moment it would all fall apart.

Karma got up, nudging Eve toward the hallway and into the video game room with Sheena and the boys.

"Go chill in there with Sheena," Karma said, nodding toward the open doorway. "I'll be there in a bit."

"Come on, darling, let's have a drink," Sheena coaxed.

Eve hesitated in the doorway, casting an uncertain glance back at Karma before shuffling into the game room. Karma watched her go, a flicker of concern crossing her face as Eve disappeared into the chaos of flashing screens and thumping music. She waited a beat, then turned and returned to Cole, her eyes dilating like a snake ready to strike.

Karma shut the door firmly inside the bedroom, shutting out the blasts of digital gunfire and muffled noise from the other room. Silence wrapped around them, tense and thick. Cole stood by the coffee table, where he'd laid out the gear with meticulous precision, almost ritualistic in its order. Karma's gaze swept over the setup, her heart pounding faster.

She reached for a worn leather belt and wrapped it tightly around her upper arm, clenching her fist to bring up a vein. She kept her focus steady, searching for the right spot, then biting her lip as the dull needle finally broke her skin. Her jaw tightened as she pressed down on the plunger, sending the liquid burning into her bloodstream. A warm numbness washed over her, each pulse beat pulling her further from her problems.

Minutes blurred as the high took hold, pulling them both into a fog. Karma's face turned pale, her skin waxy. Her eyes drifted shut, and she crumpled to the floor. Cole followed, sliding down beside her with a dull thud, his face pressed into the filthy carpet as the drugs took over.

They sprawled on the floor, the world fading away, leaving only the sluggish rise and fall of their labored breaths. Suddenly, Karma lurched forward, a guttural sound escaping her lips. "Uggggghhhh…!" She heaved, vomit splattering onto the bed, trickling down to stain the carpet. The sour taste lingered on her tongue as she wiped her mouth and straightened up, her hollow gaze sweeping over the mess.

The only thing she knew for sure was that she was fucking wasted.

GREEKTOWN
AGSC
ATHENS GREEK SOCIAL CLUB

CHAPTER 19

GREEKTOWN BALTIMORE

In the heart of Greektown, Baltimore, bordered by Lombard Street to the north, O'Donnell Street to the south, and Haven to the west, stood the Athens Greek Social Club— a quiet, smoke-filled corner of the city where deals and decisions were made behind closed doors. Inside, four old Greek men sat at a heavy wooden table tucked into a shadowed corner. It was the kind of place where every detail carried weight, and every quiet gesture meant more than words.

Theo sat back in his chair, his hands marked with age, a cigar smoldering in the corner of his mouth, casting a faint glow in the dim room. Vic sat across from him, his eyes scanning the space, his presence solid, tempered by years of experience.

A quiet but palpable menace seemed to settle around him. Flanking Theo and Vic, two henchmen stood silently, their loyalty written in their stances, every muscle alert.

Sebastian, the youngest of their crew, carefully balanced a tray of drinks as he threaded his way through the tables. The quiet clink of glasses broke the thick silence as he set them down with precision, each drink placed exactly right. As he stepped back, the room seemed to still, the regular murmurs of the club fading as the four men leaned in, ready to talk.

Vic cleared his throat, his gravelly voice cutting through the smoke-laden air. "We've been through this before," he said, his words weighted. "She's gone back to that scumbag's place—the same one we had to drag her out of last time." His voice held a sharp edge, reflecting his growing impatience.

The club's dim lighting cast heavy shadows on their faces, adding to the atmosphere as the men absorbed Vic's words. He leaned back, his fingers brushing through his graying hair as he visualized the plan, piecing together Karmella's usual haunts. He knew her patterns all too well and sensed that this low-life boyfriend's place was exactly where she would be.

"This time," Vic said slowly, his tone turning cold, "I want these guys taught a lesson."

Theo took a slow sip of his drink, the ice clinking in the glass, before nodding in agreement. "So, you two," he gestured toward the henchmen, "are going to head over there and bring Karmella home." He spoke with calm authority, as if laying down a simple truth.

Vic's patience snapped, and he slammed his hand down on the table, causing the glasses to rattle, the echo cutting through the silence. Everyone's attention turned sharply to him.

Agapios, unfazed, raised an eyebrow at Vic, still chewing a mouthful of food. "Relax, Vic," he mumbled between bites, "We'll handle it." His tone was steady, unaffected, like he was stating an obvious fact.

Leaning back, Theo exhaled a cloud of cigar smoke, watching Vic with mild amusement. "They'll take care of it, Vic. No need to worry," he added, his eyes gleaming with a hint of satisfaction.

Vic threw him a sharp look, his frustration barely contained, but Theo's smirk didn't waver. Markos, who had been mostly quiet, nodded in agreement, his focus shifting back to the food, as though the tension around him didn't exist.

Agapios, still unruffled, popped another bite into his mouth, his expression unchanged. "Come on, Vic, you know Agapios has got it," Theo said with a lazy chuckle, savoring the moment.

Agapios grinned, finally swallowing his bite. "No need to rush. We'll get it done," he said, his voice laced with easy confidence.

Vic's hands clenched under the table as he took a slow, steadying breath, fighting to keep his composure. "I can't believe I have to deal with this nonsense," he muttered.

Theo, enjoying the moment, leaned forward with a mischievous glint in his eye. "Vic, my friend," he said in a low, smooth tone, "relax."

KARMA AND EVE

oh
shit ?!

CHAPTER 20

INSIDE THE VOID

Jackson led Eve away from the others, the faint strumming of a guitar fading as they left behind the buzz of video games and the sharp, acrid scent of crystal meth burning in the next room. He nudged her into his room, closing the door with a quiet click. Light filtered through the tie-dyed sheets draped across the walls, casting a kaleidoscope of muted colors that seemed to ripple in the shadows.

"You into the Grateful Dead?" he asked, his voice low, almost conspiratorial.

Eve shook her head, her curiosity piqued. "Never heard of them," she replied.

"What?!" Jackson nearly jumped out of his skin. "Are you kidding me?"

Eve stepped further into the room, her eyes scanning the chaotic scene. The remnants of last night's party were scattered everywhere: drug paraphernalia, discarded clothes, and vinyl records strewn across the floor. Jackson moved to the corner and put on a record; the needle scratched lightly before the Grateful Dead's music filled the air.

He approached her with a smirk, leaning in close, and kissed her. At first, she stiffened, her body tense and uncertain. Still, she soon relaxed, intoxicated by the atmosphere, allowing his hands to roam freely over her. "Mmm," Eve moaned, their lips locked. His hands moved over her small breasts, then grabbed her bony hips.

"I want you to fuck me," she whispered, taking control.

Jackson's breathing quickened. He yanked her top over her head, but she caught his hands, holding them firm. Her eyes were dark and intense, and her arm trembled.

"In my ass," she said, voice steady. "I don't do it in my vagina."

She turned around, bent over, slid her panties down below her thighs to the floor, and stepped out of them.

Jackson yanked down his pants and underwear, gripped her hips, and thrust himself between her cheeks, pushing into her tight, unyielding body. He pumped with urgency, the meth coursing through his veins, amplifying every sensation.

"Yes, yes... uh, ungh, ungh, uh... uh... AUGH..." Eve moaned, her voice trembling with a mix of pleasure and pain.

"F-FUCK, it feels so intense," Jackson gasped, his face flushed, lost in the high.

Eve looked back at him, her eyes wide, tears welling and glistening on her cheeks. "Harder!" she cried out. "Please, harder!"

Jackson's rhythm quickened, each thrust more forceful than the last. "Oh God, it feels so fucking good," he groaned, his voice raw.

"Yes, yes… uh, uh, ungh… AUGH…" she continued, her voice hoarse with intensity.

His thrusts grew frantic, and suddenly, he felt the familiar surge building. "I'm gonna cum!" he shouted, pulling out too quickly. His shaft bent awkwardly, and he cried out in pain, his cum spurting out in a sudden, uncontrolled arc.

"Aughh! Owww!" He grimaced, his face twisting in agony as he clutched himself. Eve watched, rubbing herself out, turning to look at him, still panting. She reached out, but he slapped her hand away.

"Fuck, I think I broke my dick," he yelled, stepping back, holding himself in pain.

"Goddamn it."

Jackson massaged his throbbing shaft, his pants pooled around his ankles, looking disheveled and foolish.

Eve continued to rub her cooch and quickly brought herself to climax, her legs and ass shuttering.

"Ohhhhhhhhh…. Fuuuucccckkk.." she moaned in ecstasy.

She coughed, cleared her throat, gathered herself together, and took a breath. Slowly, Eve stood up, pulling her cotton underwear and regaining her composure.

"Are you okay?" she asked.

"No, I'm not fucking okay," he snapped, his voice strained.

The doorbell rang, a loud, persistent "Buzz, buzz" echoing in the room. Followed by a pounding on the door—thump, thump, thump.

Jackson's head jerked up, eyes wide.

"Now who the fuck is that?"

He quickly pulled up his pants, zipping them over his hairy calves and bony knees, then yanked a tie-dyed T-shirt over his head. Still adjusting, he moved toward the door, his movements jittery, fueled by the high.

"Owwww, goddamn it," he muttered, hobbling down the corridor, nursing his broken dick.

The group in the other room remained oblivious, engrossed in their own entertainment. Sheena was busy giving the two dudes blowjobs while she sprawled across the couch, and they continued to play video games.

Jackson, looking worse for wear, stumbled toward the front door. He snagged a golf club from the corner, letting it dangle casually from his hand as the pounding persisted— thump, thump, thump. With a sudden burst of energy, he yanked the door open. Marko and Agapios stood at the doorstep, their faces stern and eyes flashing with menace.

"Is Karmela here?" Marko demanded.

"Who?" Jackson shot back, his tone dripping with mockery. "Karmela Papadakis, dipshit," Agapios snarled, stepping in closer. Jackson straightened, squaring his shoulders and tightening his grip on a golf club.

"What the hell do you want?" he sneered.

The two men exchanged a quick glance before Agapios lunged forward, clamping a hand around Jackson's throat in a steel grip, slamming him against the wall.

"Where the hell is Karmela, you piece of shit?" he growled, his voice vibrating with rage as the walls seemed to shake with the force of his grip.

Marko moved in, delivering a vicious slap across Jackson's face, then drove a knee into his stomach. Without missing a beat, he grabbed Jackson by the collar, yanking him up and pinning him against the flimsy, painted wall. He pulled a Beretta from his waistband and pressed it against Jackson's forehead. Panic flooded Jackson's face, his raised hands trembling, a thin line of blood trickling from his lip.

From the hallway, Eve could see everything. She froze, watching fear etched into Jackson's features, his hands weakly attempting to shield himself.

"Hey, dumbass, where is she?" Marko shouted, pressing the gun harder into Jackson's forehead. "If I have to ask again, it'll be with the trigger pulled."

Glen stumbled out of the video game room, still high and blinking into the scene unfolding. "What the—" he started, but a punch knocked him to the floor, unconscious.

"Where's Karma?" they demanded, but Glen lay motionless on the dirty carpet.

Eve gasped, ducking back and darting toward the other bedroom. She knocked rapidly but softly on the door, her whisper urgent and trembling.

"Karma... Karma... Karma!"

CHAPTER 21

HOUSE OF NO ESCAPE

Eve continued banging on the door, her urgency intensifying with each knock. Cole jolted awake, his head moving from side to side, his eyes wide as he quickly assessed his surroundings.

"What the fuck!"

He touched his arms and torso as if confirming he was still intact, then glanced over to see Karma sprawled out on the bed beside him, face buried in the pillow, oblivious to the world.

The banging on the door brought him fully into the moment.

"Karma?" he called softly, nudging her shoulder.

The persistent pounding on the other side of the door lingered, echoing through the quiet room.

"Come in," Cole barked, pulling himself together as Eve slipped inside, worry etched into her face. She hurried to

Karma's side, kneeling by the mattress.

"Karma, get up," Eve urged, tapping her cheek. "Get up!" she repeated, pulling on her arm as the distant shouts and heavy footsteps grew louder from down the hall.

Karma stirred, blinking as she surfaced from sleep, her face marked with red lines from the pillow. "What... huh? What's going on?"

"There are guys here looking for you," Eve replied urgently, pushing Karma upright.

"What? Who?

Cole was already up, grabbing a baseball bat from beside the door. His body was tense, and he was ready to confront whoever had invaded their place.

"I'll handle it," he said; he disappeared into the hallway, bat in hand.

Karma, still groggy, shook herself awake. She threw on her pants, grabbed her shirt from the floor, and pulled it over her head. Her hand instinctively went to the gun lying next to her. Feeling the cool metal, she picked it up and tucked it into her waistband, heart pounding. She hadn't told Cole she had the gun, but there was no time for second-guessing.

Cole crept forward, spotting Agapios just as he reached the hallway. With a swift swing, he slammed the bat into Agapios's head, dislocating his jaw and splitting his forehead open as blood streamed down. "Ahhh!" BAM.

A gunshot is fired, and Marko, standing nearby, shoots Cole square in the chest.

"He shot me! He shot me!" Cole screamed, clutching his chest as blood pooled, soaking his shirt.

Karma seized her moment and pulled the trigger, her shot finding its mark in Marko's neck. His head jolted back, blood spraying as he crumpled against a stack of boxes.

BAM. BAM. He fired two shots blindly before his arm went limp, the gun slipping from his fingers.

Smoke curled up from Karma's gun as she took in the blood-splattered scene, her pulse racing. A shot whizzed past her, close enough to make her duck back instinctively, the air thick with tension and the metallic scent of gunpowder.

"Go, go, go!" she yelled to Eve, ducking back into the room.

Karma rushed to the window, unsnapping the lock and lifting it open, the cool air hitting her face.

"Let's go. Out, now. Come on," Karma urged, motioning to Eve, who was frozen in fear.

Karma grabbed Cole's stash from the floor, stuffing it into her pockets before helping Eve toward the window.

"Eve, go. Jump."

One by one, they scrambled through, landing on the gravel below. Eve steadied Karma as they regained their balance, adrenaline pounding in their ears.

"Bam, bam!" More gunshots erupted from inside. Without looking back, they bolted across the yard, cut through the front lawn, and sprinted down the street toward the van, hearts racing with every step.

A small group had gathered on the sidewalk across the street, staring at the house. They watched as Karma and Eve ran from the side of the building and down the street.

"Are you okay?" a man in shorts and a T-shirt called out, his voice edged with concern, but they ignored him and dived straight into the stolen van.

"Call the cops!" an overweight woman in a floral muumuu screeched, her voice shrill and panicked, slicing through the morning air.

Inside the house, Marko lay unconscious in a pool of blood. Agapios, holding a gun, shouted orders at the other kids in the room. Sheena lay dead a few feet away, a bullet wound between her eyes, blood staining her face—she'd been caught in the crossfire and not even had a chance to scream.

"Don't fucking move, assholes," Agapios shouted, his thick Greek accent harsh, the command hanging in the silence.

KARMA AND EVE

FLORIDA

CHAPTER 22

FALLING OFF THE MAP

The keys rattled in Karma's hand as she jammed one into the ignition. She twisted, and the engine snarled to life, reverberating through the van. The dashboard light flickered, then settled into a dim amber glow as the rusted engine growled like a caged beast.

Without hesitation, she stomped on the gas. The engine roared louder, and the van shuddered under the strain, its metallic growl filling the air with a raw, restless energy. Outside, people edged closer, gathering around the van, their eyes fixed on the scene.

"Go, get outta here," Eve urged. "Those people are gonna do something."

As the van idled, it emitted a few rough coughs and sputters. A cloud of black smoke burst from the exhaust, blurring the surroundings before it settled into a rough rhythm.

Karma yanked the gearshift into reverse and quickly

backed up.

THUD.

"We hit something!" Eve cried, grabbing Karma's arm.

Karma craned her neck out the window, her breath catching as she looked back. There, crumpled beneath the bumper, lay Henry—one of the neighbors—his body a broken shadow against the asphalt.

"Shit!" Karma shouted, shoving the van into drive. Another man darted in front of the van, his arms up, frantically waving. "Stop! You just hit someone—STOP!" he screamed.

Karma locked eyes with him, her face hard. Without a second thought, she slammed on the gas, and the van shot forward, the engine roaring as it plowed into him. The sickening thud of his body under the wheels sent a jolt through the van. Eve clung to her seat while Karma gritted her teeth, the sharp taste of blood filling her mouth. Her hands gripped the steering wheel, knuckles white, as they sped away, leaving chaos behind them.

Inside, the silence was thick. Karma's jaw was clenched as she gnawed her bottom lip, her thoughts racing. Eve stared out the window, eyes lost in the passing landscape, her mind somewhere distant. Every so often, Karma glanced over, trying to read her expression.

"Give me a smoke," Karma muttered.

Eve turned to Karma, her bloodshot, glassy eyes reflecting a hollow, haunted expression. Her fingers shook as she reached for the crumpled cigarette pack on the dashboard, fumbling one out and handing it over.

"Light it," Karma ordered her voice hard, leaving no room for argument.

"What do you think happened to your boyfriend?" Eve asked, her tone uncertain.

"I don't want to talk about it." Karma brushed her off, looking straight ahead.

"Don't you care?" Eve asked, puzzled by Karma's detached response.

"No... We weren't that close. Stop talking about it."

"Ok, alright." Eve turned to the window, watching the world blur past.

"Where are we going?" Eve's question broke the silence, her voice cutting through the thick tension. The drugs were wearing off, and the harsh reality began to sharpen around them.

"Florida," Karma muttered, sliding the gun into the glove box. For a brief moment, the tension eased slightly.

The tires hummed steadily against the asphalt, a dull drone that did little to calm the anxiety simmering beneath Karma's surface. Her grip tightened on the steering wheel, knuckles white, as her mind raced through what to do next.

She reached over to the dashboard, brushing her fingers against the cracked radio knobs. She flicked it on without a word, static hissing through the speakers before settling into a faint tune. She twisted the dial, searching for something to fill the silence. Eve sat quietly in the passenger seat, pale and withdrawn, staring out the window. Karma flipped through stations—stopping briefly on a classical station, then settling on a talk show with a sigh of frustration.

"And now, an important announcement for residents in the Maryland, Delaware, and Washington, D.C. areas," the announcer's crisp, authoritative voice filled the van. "Police are currently searching for two young women who escaped from the Helmbrook Mental Hospital earlier today. The pair are considered dangerous and should not be approached. If you have any information, please get in touch with your local authorities immediately."

"Shit," Karma muttered as she turned up the volume on the radio. Her breath caught in her throat as she glanced in the rearview mirror, half-expecting to see flashing lights behind them. The empty road stretched out ahead, but each word from the radio landed in her stomach like a punch.

Eve clutched her seatbelt, wide-eyed. "Karma..." she whispered, her voice barely audible.

"Shut up," Karma snapped, her pulse pounding as panic clawed at the edges of her control. She wanted to change the station, to drown out the voice forecasting their fate, but she couldn't. She needed to hear every word.

Authorities are urging residents, especially those in rural areas, to stay vigilant. The two women are believed to be traveling on foot or in a stolen vehicle. They are described as approximately 5'5" and 5'7" tall, with one having dark hair and the other having blonde hair. They were last seen near the hospital in Delaware and may be headed towards Baltimore or Washington, D.C. Anyone who notices any suspicious activity is encouraged to contact the police immediately.

A chill crept up Karma's spine as sweat gathered on her skin. The description was vague for now, but it wouldn't stay that way. Sooner or later, someone would piece it together. Time was slipping, and their chances of escape grew slimmer every second. The clock was ticking, and they were running out of hiding places.

The announcer's voice faded into static, replaced by a commercial jingle. Karma snapped off the radio and glanced at Eve, who looked like she was on the verge of tears, her body trembling with fear.

Karma's voice was low and steady, though she felt anything but calm. "We'll drive for a bit," she said. "Find somewhere to lay low until we figure out what to do next."

"Ok," Eve muttered, barely audible. Her face was streaked with sweat and grime, and her shoulders slumped as she stared blankly ahead. The weight of everything seemed to have finally sunk in.

Karma's face was pale, her skin greasy, and dark circles clung beneath her eyes, giving her a hollow, exhausted look. The spark that usually lit her eyes had faded, leaving them dull and distant. Her cracked and dry lips pressed into a thin line as she stared out, her expression heavy with the weight of too many bad decisions piling up like debris.

After about half an hour, the van sputtered, the engine coughing and rattling before stalling completely. Karma's heart dropped as the power faded, and the dashboard lights flickered before going dark. She pulled over, and with a final groan, the van came to a dead stop.

Karma leaned back in her seat, her breath coming in short, shallow bursts as she tried to figure out their next move. The dull, orange glow of early morning barely pierced the thick fog hanging over the road, adding to the growing sense of unease. Without warning, Eve flung open the passenger door and stumbled out of the van. She barely made it to the side of the road before doubling over, retching violently onto the gravel. The sound of her vomiting echoed in the stillness, harsh and guttural, cutting through the silence like a knife.

Karma watched her for a moment, emotions churning in turmoil. She reached for the flip phone she had taken from the hospital attendant, flipping it open with a snap. Her fingers moved automatically, scrolling through the phone's contents while she waited for Eve to recover.

As she scrolled, a series of photos filled the small screen. Karma's breath caught as she stared at the images—pictures of Eve, her face twisted in fear. In some of the photos, Karma could see herself in the background, passed out, unaware of the nightmare unfolding beside her. Eve's eyes in the images were dilated with terror, her body clearly manipulated into degrading positions. Karma's heart pounded, her skin prickling as the photos shifted to show her face. She was unconscious, her body positioned in ways that made her stomach churn, her vulnerability displayed without her knowledge. In some frames, Eve could be seen in the background, her expression veering from horrified to hollow and defeated.

A violent wave of anger surged through Karma. The phone slipped from her grasp, clattering onto the dashboard as her hands turned into fists. The realization of what had happened while she was unconscious hit her like a punch to the gut, and an overwhelming rage, unlike anything she had ever experienced boiled up inside her. Just then, Eve stumbled back into the van, wiping her mouth with the back of her hand. Her face was pale, her eyes glassy, and she was exhausted. She looked at Karma, sensing something was wrong, but before she could speak, Karma turned to her, eyes blazing.

"What the hell is this?" Karma spat, shoving the phone in Eve's face.

Eve blinked, her eyes widening as she saw the images on the screen. "Karma, I—" she started, but Karma cut her off.

"You let this happen?" Karma's voice rose, trembling with anger.

"You let him do this while I was passed out? You didn't

stop him?"

Eve shook her head frantically, tears welling up. "Karma, I didn't want to—he forced me! I couldn't stop him!" she pleaded, her voice breaking with desperation.

But Karma was beyond reason, her rage blinding her to everything else. "You expect me to believe that?" she shouted.

"You let him do this to you? You didn't even try to stop it?"

Eve recoiled as if slapped. "I couldn't stop him, Karma! He was stronger—I tried, but I couldn't!" she cried, voice shaking with fear.

Karma's vision blurred with fury, her mind spinning with betrayal and hurt. "You let him touch me! You let him do those things to you, and you didn't fight back!" she screamed, lunging at Eve, grabbing her by the shoulders.

Eve tried to push her away, but Karma's grip was a vice.

"Karma, stop! Please, listen to me!" she begged, tears streaming down her face.

"I didn't have a choice!"

The van shook as they struggled, their bodies clashing in a chaotic fight. Karma's fists lashed out in blind fury, her punches uncontrolled and unpredictable. Eve fought to protect herself, desperately trying to fend off Karma's rage.

"You let him do this to me!" Karma screamed.

Realizing she was losing the fight, Eve shoved Karma back long enough to scramble for the door. She tumbled out of the van, her feet hitting the gravel as she stumbled to the side of the road. Karma was on her instantly, following her into the cool air, fists clenched, her face a mask of fury.

"Why didn't you fight back?" Karma screamed, advancing on

Eve, her fists clenched tight.

"I couldn't!" Eve shot back, her voice cracking as she stumbled back. "He was going to hurt me … Karma! I couldn't stop

him!"

"You always have a choice!" Karma yelled, throwing a wild punch that landed on Eve's shoulder, sending her stumbling backward.

Fear surged through Eve as she realized she was cornered. Her hand shot into her pocket, trembling as she pulled out a small, crude shank—a jagged shard of metal wrapped in cloth. She thrusted it out between them, the sharp edge glinting faintly in the grey light creeping over the horizon.

"Karma, stop!" Eve shouted, her voice shaking, her tears cutting streaks through the grime on her face. "I don't want to hurt you, but I will if I have to! Please, just stop!"

Karma's bloodshot eyes fixed on the weapon in Eve's trembling hand. For a moment, she stilled, her chest rising and falling with each jagged breath, the air catching harshly in her throat. Then, slowly, a cruel smirk twisted her lips. "That's supposed to scare me?" she growled, her voice low and edged with disdain.

Before Eve could react, Karma lunged. Her hand shot out, knocking the shank from Eve's grip. The crude blade clattered to the asphalt as Karma's other fist swung up, connecting with Eve's jaw and sending her reeling.

"You think this is my first fight, cunt?" Karma snarled, her voice breaking under the weight of her fury. She grabbed Eve by the front of her shirt and slammed her against the side of the van, the dull clang ringing out across the empty road.

Eve's hands shot up to defend herself, but Karma was relentless. A punch to the ribs, an elbow to the temple—it wasn't clean or calculated, just raw, ugly rage.

"You had a choice! You always had a choice!" Karma spat, her voice cracking.

Eve crumpled to the ground, curling into herself, her hands up to shield her face. "Karma, please! Stop!" she begged, her voice desperate.

Karma loomed over her, with her fists clenched and breath coming in hard bursts. For a moment, it seemed like she might hit her again, her body coiled tight with fury. But then, slowly, her arms fell to her sides. The tension unraveled as the adrenaline bled away, leaving her spent and hollow.

Eve remained on the ground, her shoulders trembling with silent sobs. "I'm sorry," she whispered, her voice so faint it barely rose above the stillness of the road.

Karma took a shaky step back, staring down at Eve. Her

own knuckles throbbed, the skin split and bleeding, but she barely noticed. Her mind was struggling to sift through the wreckage of her anger, the betrayal still sharp, raw, and unhealed.

The van sat in the background, silent and lifeless, its battered frame catching the first rays of morning light. Karma's chest heaved as she fought to catch her breath. The adrenaline slowly fading and leaving her feeling hollow.

Eve sat up, cradling her ribs, her eyes wide and filled with something between terror and resignation.

"I didn't know what else to do," she stammered, her voice breaking. "I tried to fight him—God, I swear I did. But he was stronger, and he … he threatened me. He threatened us."

Karma said nothing, her face blank but her jaw tight.

Eve wiped at her face with trembling hands, smearing the tears and dirt into a messy blur. "I promise you can trust me, Karma," she whispered. "I didn't want any of this."

Karma snorted bitterly, "Trust you? That's a joke." She leaned back against the van, sliding down until she was sitting on the cold asphalt, her arms draped over her knees. "You don't get to play the victim here, Eve. You made your choices."

Eve nodded, swallowing hard. "I know."

They sat there for a long moment, the silence heavy and unmoving, hanging between them like a storm about to break. The tension didn't shatter; it unraveled slowly, like an old rope fraying to its last threads.

Eve glanced at the shank lying a few feet away, the jagged edge gleaming faintly. She reached for it, carefully, watching Karma's face. When Karma didn't move, Eve tucked it away, the motion tentative, almost like a truce.

Finally, Karma looked over at her, her voice low. "If you pull that on me again, I'll kill you. Don't think I won't."

Eve flinched but nodded. "I won't," she said, her voice barely audible.

"It was just pictures," she added, her gaze fixed on the ground. "He never raped you." Her voice cracked, but she forced the words out, as if saying them might somehow lessen the weight they carried.

Karma let out a harsh laugh, bitter and humorless.

"Like that makes it better." She leaned her head back against the van, closing her eyes. "I don't wanna talk about it anymore."

The dawn crept in, the grey light of morning stretching across the empty road. The air was heavy, still, offering no comfort, no relief.

Bruised, battered, and bleeding, they sat at the side of the road, two broken pieces trying to hold together the fragile alliance they'd just forged. The van was dead, their options dwindling, and the uncertain path ahead stretched out before them like a promise and a threat.

Eve glanced at the van, then back at Karma.

"What do we do now?" she asked.

Karma let out a long sigh, her shoulders sagging under the crushing weight of withdrawal and sheer exhaustion.

"We walk," she muttered, her voice flat. "We'll find somewhere to lay low, regroup, figure things out."

Eve nodded, though the thought of trekking down the empty road filled her with dread. But she knew Karma was right; they had no other choice.

They began walking, their footsteps crunching on the gravel as they left the van behind, disappearing into the unknown. The fog that clung to the ground seemed to follow them, thickening with each step as if intent on swallowing them whole. The road stretched endlessly before them, a gray ribbon winding through the mist and leading into emptiness.

Karma walked a few steps ahead, her movements stiff and mechanical, like she was dragging herself through quicksand. Behind her, Eve lagged, her mind spinning with anxious thoughts about what might come next. Neither spoke, their footsteps crunching softly against the dirt road. They moved like ghosts, hollowed out and aimless, as if the weight of everything had stripped them down to nothing but motion.

The fog began to lift, unveiling fields of tall grass rippling softly in the breeze. The scene felt almost serene, a sharp contrast to the chaos that had consumed them moments before.

Hours passed, and the road remained empty, except for an

occasional bird flying from the fields. They continued on, their bodies growing more exhausted with each mile.

Finally, they reached a small, dilapidated gas station. The building's paint was peeling in long, jagged strips, and the windows were thick with grime. Out front, a rusted pickup truck slumped on flat tires, its hood dented and speckled with bullet holes.

Karma glanced at Eve, who gave a curt nod. Without a word, they approached cautiously, the desolate air pressing down around them. They peered through the filthy windows, straining to see inside, but the dim light revealed little beyond shadows and debris.

Karma tugged on the door, but it wouldn't budge. "Great," she muttered under her breath, frustration flashing across her face. She rammed her shoulder against it, and with a metallic groan, the door gave way, swinging open with a screech that echoed into the empty fields.

Inside, the air was stale and heavy, reeking faintly of mildew, ash, piss and shit. The walls were smeared with faded graffiti—crude symbols, names, and curses spray-painted in erratic scrawls. The shelves were barren, their contents long scavenged.

Near the corner of the room, a makeshift campfire blackened the cracked tile floor, its charred remains stomped out and cold.

Eve stepped over a pile of shattered glass.

Karma scanned the room with sharp eyes. A faded map hung crookedly behind the counter, its edges curling with age.

"It's not much, but it'll do for now," Karma said, her voice low and tired.

They sat on the dusty floor, backs against the graffiti-covered wall. Eve pulled her knees to her chest, staring at the remnants of the campfire as if trying to picture who had been here before them. Karma leaned her head back, closing her eyes for a moment, her body aching from exhaustion.

The silence stretched between them. Finally, Karma sat forward. "We rest, but not for long," she said, her tone firm.

"We can't stay here long."

Eve nodded silently, glancing at the shattered windows and the sagging roof, feeling the vulnerability in every shadow of the place. Whatever safety the gas station offered was temporary, at best.

Karma sat with her head resting back, her bandaged wrists limp at her sides. After a moment, she reached into her pocket, her fingers brushing against the small stash she had lifted from Cole early. She put some of the powder on the back of her hand, hesitated, glanced at Eve sleeping, and snorted the powder in one quick motion. The effects hit her brain almost instantly.

Time blurred, and Karma's eyes fluttered shut. Both of them drifted into an uneasy sleep, their bodies slumped against the wall, their minds too fucked up to dream.

A sound outside—the faint rustle of wind through the grass—jerked Karma awake. Her heart skipped as she rubbed at her face, her body stiff and aching. Still high as fuck, she glanced at Eve, who was still sleeping, curled into herself like a

child.

"Eve," Karma muttered, nudging her leg with her boot. "Wake up. We gotta move."

Eve stirred groggily, blinking at Karma before pulling herself upright with a groan. The stiffness in her joints and the cold of the day made every movement feel like a chore.

Without a word, they hauled themselves to their feet and stepped through the door, back onto the barren road.

The world felt unhinged, a chaotic blur as the road stretched ahead of them, endless and uncertain, like a question that could never be answered. Together, battered but unbroken, they kept moving forward.

Just two fucking psychos.

End of Book One

213

EVE
BOOK 2
STORY D. McLOUGHLIN   ART AcCABLE

EVE

BOOK 2

"Eve would only fuck in the butt. She wanted to stay a virgin as long as she could, and men never minded jumping the shark"

Scan QR code for upcoming books, special offers, and swag for anyone that has purchased a book from Crimson Pine Publishing.